Martin and I were parked out near Mill Pond sitting in his pick-up. If you must know, we had kissed occasionally.... Anyway, after a moment, I faced him and played my first card. "You know," I said, "your dad's upset a lot of people with this book business. To some people, what he's trying to do seems like censorship."

"It is," Martin replied simply. "I agree. I've told him so, too. But it didn't do much good." He paused. "I liked the book myself."

"Me too. I thought it said something important about the little guy versus the big ones."

"Which brings us back to my esteemed father," Martin said regretfully.

"Except in this case, the little guy is my little sister. And she's going to fight your father till the end."

"That doesn't sound like a very fair match," Martin allowed.

"Don't be too sure," I cautioned him. "She's just getting started."

**4,500,000 copies of John Neufeld's young adult novels in print.**

# A Small Civil War

## by JOHN NEUFELD

FAWCETT JUNIPER • NEW YORK

For
Alice, Bob, and Jane,
who never stopped believing.

A Fawcett Juniper Book
Published by Ballantine Books
Copyright © 1982 by John Neufeid

ISBN 0-449-70082-8

Printed in Canada

First Fawcett Juniper Edition: April 1982
First Ballantine Books Edition: April 1983

# 1.

Sometimes you never even hear the "click" of a pistol being cocked.

"Did you read the paper today?" my sister Georgia asked at dinner. Her reedy voice is appealing when life is calm; when it's not, it is unbelievably grating.

"What in particular, dear?" asked my mother in return.

"Pass the gravy," Jonny said, eleven years of manners forgotten.

"Please," prompted Daddy.

"Please," Jonny echoed obediently.

"About Mr. Brady," Georgia pressed on, her voice still at moderate pitch, the glassware in the house safe for another few minutes.

"What about him?" asked my father somberly.

"He wants to investigate *The Grapes of Wrath*," Georgia answered. "I mean, can you believe it?"

"Why does he want to do that, dear?" asked Mother, who was really, just then, not paying strict attention. I, on the other hand, seated directly across from Georgia, could see the flush begin to creep from her throat to her cheeks.

"God only knows!" Georgia said exasperatedly.

"Georgia!" my father scowled.

"Excuse me, but I mean it. After all, what on earth can be wrong with such an ancient book? How dirty can it be?"

"Is that what Councilman Brady says?" asked Mother. "That it's dirty?"

"He finds it 'objectionable.'" Georgia made her voice deep and ominous. "He thinks parts of it are 'un-American.'"

"As I remember it," said Mother thoughtfully, "it's just a terribly sad story of people during the Depression, fighting to get along, to put food on the table, to get to California where they think life will be better."

"That doesn't sound so awful to me," Georgia allowed.

"You haven't read it?" Daddy asked.

Georgia shook her head, her curls waving from one side of her forehead to the other. She looks a bit like a late Victorian street urchin out of Charles Dickens: straight, sharp nose, brightly colored cheeks, wide brown eyes. "We don't get it until tenth grade," she explained. "Matt Brady's in tenth grade. That's how his father found it."

"Perhaps Councilman Brady has a point," my father suggested. "Maybe parts of it are rough."

"Who cares?" Georgia shot back, her eyes growing huge. "Life is rough, parts of it."

My father smiled softly. He has a nice smile, but odd since the corners of his mouth turn down instead of up, and he presses his lips together a bit.

"Don't you see what this could mean?" Georgia demanded suddenly, her voice rising in disbelief that we could all be so dense.

"What?" asked Mother.

"Censorship!" Georgia cried out at the top of her lungs, throwing both arms straight out from her sides. "Censorship!" she shouted again. "Dictatorship!"

"All that here in sleepy little Owanka," my father teased.

Georgia's eyes clouded and she dropped her arms dramatically to her sides. A good many of her gestures are like that, dramatic, overstated, ill-suited to someone who barely has to wear a bra. "What makes you think it couldn't happen here?" she asked angrily. "Not everything bad comes from the outside, you know."

"Whoa," said my father gently. "Easy there. I think maybe we need to know a little more about all this."

"I don't see why." Georgia pouted. "A man says that *he* thinks other people shouldn't read a certain book. That man is on the City Council, which also controls the School Board. That man has some influence."

"So?" Mother encouraged.

"So, you can see for yourself where this could lead." Georgia was nearly breathless. "What's to keep him from banning that book, from suggesting later that another one is just as bad, that *it* be removed from school, or maybe even hundreds of other books? Whole libraries could be destroyed!"

"Pass the butter," said Jonny.

"This affects you, too, twerp!" Georgia shot at him.

"Your tongue, please, miss," said Father sternly. "I won't warn you again."

"Well, it does!" Georgia insisted. "By the time Jonny gets to high school, there may not be anything left on the shelves there he's allowed to read."

"I can write my own books," said Jonny confidently.

"Don't you think, Georgia dear," my mother said, putting a soft hand on one of Jonny's to quiet him, "that you're firing early, maybe even before you can see the target? Just wondering aloud whether one particular book is suitable for young people doesn't make Mr. Brady an ogre."

Georgia put both her bony elbows on the table and

turned to face Mother. "A Nazi is more like it," she said under her breath but clearly.

My mother smiled tolerantly. "As I recall, darling," she said slowly, "that book was written and published for grown-ups. Sometimes—and I don't mean this personally, Georgia, just generally—sometimes we all assume you children are so much more adult and sophisticated than we were at your age that we forget a line does still exist between you and us."

"What on earth does that mean?" Georgia asked.

"What your mother means," Daddy explained, "is that sometimes adults, teachers, parents, overestimate the capabilities of the young."

"Do I presume," Georgia said, straightening in her chair and sitting absolutely rigid, her voice trembling, "that you mean me?"

"If the shoe fits," Jonny slipped in.

Georgia ignored him. "Well," she pressed on, facing me now across the table, "*you* read it, Ava. What did *you* think?"

I shrugged.

"Her waterlogged brain's gone dead," Georgia announced. "No connections left between thought and nerves."

I overlooked the gratuitous slur on one of my extra-curricular activities. "As a matter of fact," I said finally, "I can remember perfectly."

"And?" Georgia urged.

"There are some words in there," I said rather weakly.

"Like what?" Jonny asked eagerly.

"Never mind," Georgia said. "Go on. What else is in it?"

"You know, the usual stuff," I hedged. "A little sex, a little profanity."

"What would make it un-American?" Georgia asked.

"I don't know," I answered truthfully. "I mean, it *is* about American families, facing American problems. I don't really think it could be un-American."

"Well," said Father, reaching out to pull Jonny's plate away from his place so that he couldn't slop up more gravy with half a roll, "Fairchild Brady's always been straightforward and honest."

"With a name like that..." Georgia muttered.

"I doubt very much that whatever his reasons are," my father continued, "they pose a threat to life here in Owanka."

"That's easy for you to say," Georgia said angrily. "Your life is already half lived."

"True enough," said Daddy, the corners of his mouth turning down once again and his thin lips compressed. "And sometimes, my dear, you do not make the second half such a time of leisure and joy."

"But I'm talking about issues!" Georgia almost shrieked.

"What you're doing is judging personalities," Father argued.

"Robin would agree with me!" Georgia announced, reaching out desperately and distantly to one of our twin brothers, who had just left to start college.

"Perhaps he would," Daddy agreed. "Perhaps if we knew more about this, we'd all agree with you."

"Well, all you have to do is read the paper!"

"Let's give it another few days," Daddy suggested.

"What happens if there's nothing more in the paper?" demanded Georgia. "Suppose Brady forms a committee and they report and then act and ban the book and we know nothing about it?"

"That's not very likely, dear," my mother said. "After all, if the *Herald* wrote about it at all, they'll certainly want to follow up on it. I think that's just good journalism, don't you, Ava?"

I nodded agreeably.

"What if they forget?" asked Georgia.

"Then you do it," Jonny said quickly. "You write them about it."

"I might just do that," Georgia said.

"After all," Daddy said, "we've a free press here. That's how you learned about Mr. Brady's crusade in the first place. Be grateful."

"That's exactly what I'm talking about!" Georgia yelled at the ceiling. The chandelier (actually that makes it sound grander than it is but there's really no other word for it) swayed on its chain. "I'm trying to talk about saving the freedom of the press, the freedom of us all!"

"I don't feel threatened," my father said.

"That's how it begins," Georgia said ominously, dropping her voice again. "No one does. And then, suddenly, you wake up one day and it's too late."

"Sweetheart," my mother interjected, "what are you reading now?"

Georgia blushed.

"Well?" my mother waited.

*The Diary of Anne Frank.*"

My father's mouth twitched to repress the smile and my mother averted her eyes.

"Well, for heaven's sakes," I said, "that explains the whole thing."

"It most certainly does not!" Georgia was firm.

"Of course it does," I said. "You're all nerve ends from that, looking for oppression and disaster everywhere."

"What none of you seems to realize," Georgia said with sudden dignity, standing at her place, "is that Anne Frank aside, the kind of thing that happened years ago in Europe can happen anywhere, anytime, unless we're all determined to stand up for our rights."

"Don't forget to take something with you, dear," suggested Mother, motioning around the table so that Georgia would take a plate or two at the same time she stalked dramatically out of the room.

Incredibly, war had been declared, and none of us knew it.

# 2.

Though it was easy enough for Georgia to write the editors of the *Owanka Herald,* actually I'm the one with literary talent in our family. Myself and Robin.

The genes are probably Mother's since it is she who every Wednesday afternoon goes to the public library to spend hours there reading the Sunday *New York Times,* section by hefty section. Just as she lines us up in front of the family television set for "Masterpiece Theatre," insisting at the same time that watching a dramatization of a book is only an introduction to that book, not a replacement for the actual reading experience. Also, Mom's a member of the Book-of-the-Month Club, a primary organizer for the annual Planned Parenthood book sale, and devotes a lot of spare time and energy (and her warm alto voice) to the Owanka Renaissance Chorale. Not to mention deciding where we go on family vacations, or used to, because now that Robin and Rick are away at college, it's unlikely the seven of us are ever again going to squeeze into her station wagon to head downriver to see Mark Twain's home and museum in Hannibal, Missouri, or drive hundreds of miles to the Southwest to explore the native American cultures of the Hopis and Zunis in Arizona and New Mexico, or amble slowly along the Cum-

berland Trail or among the Smokies, up to Gettysburg
and then down again to Williamsburg on a Colonial
America swing.

To be perfectly honest, I didn't have a lot of extra
time on my hands that autumn. I had just been elected
president of the Sharks Club—a synchronized swim-
ming team we have at Owanka High which for the past
four out of five years has been Iowa state champion—
and that inspired Georgia's backhanded reference to
being waterlogged. I was on the Student Council for
the fourth year running, besides being a soloist in our
church choir and holding a part-time job on Saturday's
at Chez Elle, a boutique on the square. Apart from all
this, I had Martin Brady on my right arm (he, the
offspring of Georgia's newly discovered Satan) and
sniffing around to take my left was a new boy in school,
Darryl von Vrock.

In other words, at the start of my senior year I was
fresh and eager, feeling accomplished and hopeful and
romantic, and *on the threshold.* Bad timing; missed connections; star-crossed—for that was the year Georgia
declared war on bigotry and repression and censorship
and headed straight to disaster.

One other extracurricular activity consumed me: the
Owanka High *Hawk,* our school's weekly newspaper,
the sort of extra-credit thing that always looks so good
on college applications. I had *not* been elected editor,
which, the April before, had dented my self-esteem a
little, I admit. But I hung on and, since I did, I should try
to be honest now and report what happened in Owanka
with as little shading as possible. So, first of all, I have
to confess I missed an opportunity—perhaps *the* opportunity—to control the course of Georgia's campaign.

For it was to me, secretly, about a week later, that
she came. I was in our room at the time, studying English history, frantically trying to memorize the succes-

sion of Plantagenets and Tudors and Stuarts all the way up to Elizabeth II. We had had dinner and she and I had cleared the table and done the dishes while Mother and Daddy went next door to the Duggans' house for coffee and dessert—not to mention a few hours away from the rest of us. Jonny was in bed, I suppose, because it must have been after nine.

"Ava?" Georgia said rather tentatively as she came into the room.

I did not look up. "What?" I asked, distracted from Edwards and Anne.

"Will you do me a favor?"

"What?"

"Will you?"

"I don't operate that way," I said firmly. "Tell me first."

"Come down to the town hall tomorrow with me."

"What on earth for?" I asked, swinging around in my chair to see her stretched out on her bed, stomach down, her head propped up on her hands, staring at me. Her face was almost expressionless, as though she were afraid either to hope or to give up.

"There's a Council meeting," Georgia said quietly.

"So?"

She frowned. "Don't you remember last week, about Mr. Brady?"

"Yes, I remember. What's happening now?"

Georgia shrugged. "I don't know. That's why I want to go, to find out."

"You don't need me for that."

She smiled. Georgia has an incredibly warm, confidential welcoming smile. "I didn't say I needed you for that," she allowed. "I just thought, what with you nosing around the editor's desk at *The Hawk,* you *ought* to go for your own reasons."

"Such as?" I was curious and also, to be frank, a bit annoyed that Georgia was pushing a career on me.

"It's probably going to be a good story," Georgia said flatly. "And it's something that's going to affect your readers, you know. I mean, you've got nearly two hundred tenth-graders in school who read your stuff. It's their lives that are going to be changed."

"You've lost me," I said.

Georgia sighed, trying to cover her disappointment. (Or not trying, which is more likely.) "Don't you understand?" she asked seriously. "If Mr. Brady gets *The Grapes of Wrath* blacklisted, taken off the assigned reading list, something else has to be put in its place. Who's to decide that? If a teacher gets his hands slapped in public for recommending and insisting that his students read something subversive, how gutsy is he going to be when he has to choose another book? And who is going to pass on his selection? Will he have to submit it to the Council? Suppose he does, suppose the second book gets knocked down, too. Then what?"

"I don't know," I said. "I guess he keeps trying to find something that's OK."

Georgia shook her head and, as I recall now, a smile not unlike my father's—corners down, lips pursed— edged onto her face. "You really don't get it, do you?" she asked almost sadly. "Don't you see, Ava? There's hardly a book on earth a teacher could recommend that someone on that board couldn't find objections to."

I grinned. "Terrific," I decided. "We can all skip English then and graduate early and get on with the rest of our lives."

"That's positive drivel," Georgia said with disgust. "You've already read the book. I haven't. Jonny hasn't."

"No one's keeping you from trying," I said.

"They are, too."

"Georgia, look. If the worst happens and the book is

taken off the list, who cares? You can buy a copy of it somewhere else, at a drugstore or a bookstore or an airport. You can read it if it's so important to you."

"But that would make me feel sleazy," Georgia said. "Why should I have to sneak around and get it somewhere else if it's really harmless?"

"Isn't that what your meeting's about?" I asked. "Finding out whether or not it is harmless?"

"What this meeting is about is whether Fairchild Brady can get people worked up enough to vote him back onto the Council, only this time on the basis of fear and anger."

"Oh, Georgia, come on!"

"I'm serious!" she said, sitting up and crossing her legs on her bed. "That's exactly what he's doing. He's manipulating the whole town for his own purposes. You don't really think Mr. Brady's even read the silly book all the way through, do you?"

"I certainly hope so," I said sensibly. "Otherwise, what's all the fuss?"

"He's campaigning," Georgia said again. "That's all it is. He's trying to get in the papers and on radio or whatever."

"Well, that's easy enough," I said. "He owns the radio station."

Georgia was silent then, looking at me with a mixture of disapproval and hope. There is an earnestness about her that's appealing, no matter how confused her temporary goal is. "You want me to go to the meeting and report in *The Hawk* on the issue, is that it?"

She nodded.

I shook my head.

"But why not?" she demanded.

"Because the regular newspaper people will be there, that's why. Because *The Hawk* comes out on Thursdays and tomorrow is Tuesday, and the *Herald* will report on the meeting Wednesday. It will be old news."

"You assume everyone at school reads the *Herald?*"

"Why not? We do."

"Boy, are you gullible."

"Maybe," I admitted. "It also happens that there's a Sharks practice tomorrow that I can't miss." I paused and took a big breath. "Not to mention the fact, though of course you're too dense to understand this, that it is *Martin's* father you want to shoot down."

Georgia snorted through her nose and frowned. *Most* attractive. I keep forgetting she's only fourteen and just barely conversant with good manners or anything resembling adult behavior. Let alone the concept of loyalty. "Why not take Mother with you?" I suggested then as a sort of pacifying substitute.

"Because *you're* the one with influence, if you only realized it," Georgia said angrily, getting up then from her bed and stalking from the room. "God, you are so nearsighted I can't believe it!"

I prided myself on knowing how to manage and balance the different elements of my life. Besides, this was all Georgia's show. So I thought nothing more about her judgments and returned diligently to Mary and Elizabeth and to James, James, and George.

Maybe twenty minutes later Georgia came back into our bedroom and began to undress. She was humming a little tune under her breath but I refused to let it get to me. (You learn to do this with younger sisters, or brothers, for that matter. Once they realize they can shatter your composure, or your concentration, you're finished.) I kept my eyes closed, my book open, murmuring *Henry, Edward, Mary, Elizabeth.* I heard Georgia cross the room behind me to get to the bathroom. I heard water running, the toilet flush, more water running, and the sound of teeth being brushed.

Georgia came back into the room and passed once more behind my chair. I heard her getting into her bed and saw, from the corner of my eye, her bedside lamp switch off. There was a moment's silence.

"It's O.K.," Georgia said to me as she nestled into her pillow. "You don't have to come with me." She paused. "Robin's coming home."

# 3.

Georgia, naturally, slept soundly that night. I did not. What, I wondered, had she told Robin that would make him come home after only three and a half weeks at the university? What urgency did he understand so quickly that the rest of us missed?

Also, though I knew this was make-believe, I smiled to imagine that Georgia had used some sort of black-mail on him. Perhaps she knew something the rest of us didn't.

But I didn't have a lot of free time during the fol-lowing day to consider all this. Apart from classes and general child's play in the halls at school, my world came close to exploding as Darryl von Vrock cornered me between fifth and sixth periods at my locker to lower his head and look seductively up at me from under his heavy eyelashes to ask, "Tonight?"

I laughed. "No, not tonight."

"Tomorrow?" he suggested.

I smiled, leading him on but with no real intention of falling into his trap. After all, from what I heard and saw, Darryl was out to conquer each and every halfway decent-looking girl in school. (In my own defense, *I* am halfway decent-looking: my hair is brown and longish, falling nearly to my shoulders, straight and always clean; my eyes are clear and blue, speckled with just the tiniest golden motes; and I wear a thirty-four C, which of course doesn't hurt.)

So I smiled on, when suddenly I saw Martin Brady crossing the hallway ahead of me. He looked quickly down the row of lockers at us, and catching my attempt at Mona Lisa-ing, saw what was going on. I froze.

Darryl didn't notice. "OK, Ava, but sooner or later it's going to happen," he said in a whisper. "It's going to be wonderful."

Half of me was tempted to ask what "it" was, and half was tempted to answer my own question and say Never! But all of me felt instantly guilty and I wanted to break away from Darryl, track Martin down, and explain. I didn't. I couldn't. The bell for sixth period rang.

By the time Sharks practice was over I had completely forgotten about Georgia's troops being bussed in. But the first few minutes at our dining-room table caused my stomach to jump, to feel suddenly tender and unsettled.

"I think Georgia's absolutely right," Robin said in answer to my father's question. I looked across at him, always serious, always sensible and thoughtful. If Rick was a star, a quarterback, a forward, a pitcher, Robin was a team player, considerate, quiet, backing up every shot, every pitch, ready to save and catch and make good someone else's error.

Though he and Rick are not identical twins, there is a clear and obvious resemblance between them. Both are over six feet tall. Rick is filled out and muscular, Robin sinewy, thinner, but strong. Both have my mother's brown hair, but Robin has my father's blue eyes while Rick's are brown. Rick has a broad, open, instantaneous smile, the ability to laugh easily and sometimes to poke fun. Robin is rather slyer, slow to belittle, a little quicker to appreciate.

"So what happened?" Mother wanted to know.

"The Council approved a committee to investigate the book," Robin told her. "Not big enough, however, to allow for subcommittees or much argument."

"What do you mean?" asked Mother then.

Robin grinned. "We now have a one-man committee, and I would guess that that means the committee is pretty much under the thumb of Mr. Brady."

"Who is it?" my father asked.

Robin's grin widened. "Stanley Sopwith."

My father laughed softly.

"Still," Robin went on, "it's a long book. All old Stanley is delegated to do is examine the first parts of it, to get a general tone, I gather."

"What exactly is he looking for?" I asked.

Robin shrugged. "Primarily language, I guess. Rough language."

"Well, that's certainly there," I told him. "But so what? There's a lot of tenderness in there, too. And common sense."

Georgia swallowed her milk quickly. "They're looking for subversive ideas."

"What's being subverted?" asked Father.

"The American Way," Robin answered with another smile. "God, Country, Motherhood, Big Business, what's good for General Motors is good for America."

"Did someone actually say that?" Father asked.

Robin shook his head. "That will come, though. You can just tell, from the tone of the meeting. It's just a good thing Steinbeck wasn't black."

Georgia nodded in agreement. "That will come, too, you know. That's what Miss McCandless told me."

"Who's Miss McCandless, dear?" Mother wanted to know.

"Our librarian," Georgia replied. "I guess I forgot to mention her."

"You can't remember everything," Mother said easily. "When did you meet with her?"

"Last week."

"To talk about Mr. Brady?" asked my father.

"Not so much about him," Georgia said. "About his ideas."

"What was her reaction?" I asked.

Georgia smiled happily. "If you must know, she said that this sort of thing is far from new. From time to time it happens in different parts of the country. She's never personally been involved in a case like this, but she's read about others and," Georgia paused dramatically as she likes to do, "she thinks she knows how to handle Mr. Brady now that he's in her own backyard. She said there were lots of Fairchild Bradys peering through hedges into other people's homes and other people's business."

"She sounds prepared," Father estimated.

"She should be," Robin said.

"If you don't mind my asking," Father said then, "how is it you expect to keep up with your own schoolwork if you're running back here at every opportunity, Robin?"

"I'm not going to do that, Dad. At least, I don't think so. This time, well, Georgia needed me. I think after we organize things, she can handle everything herself, she and her friends."

"Her friends?" I was astonished. "You mean you've already started choosing sides?"

"You have to," Georgia answered somberly. "There isn't that much time. Mr. Brady wants to put the book on the ballot, and the election's less than six weeks away."

"How can he do that?" asked Jonny suddenly. "I thought the state of Iowa printed the ballots."

"It does," Robin explained. "But Mr. Brady wants an extra one, hand-printed, filled out. A referendum."

"Doesn't that cost money?" asked Father. "And wouldn't the Council have to approve the expenditure?"

"Sure," Robin replied. "But don't forget how persuasive Mr. Brady can be. After all, he's been on the Council longer than most people around here have owned their cars."

"If you two are so worked up," I said then, "how come you didn't say something at the meeting itself?"

"I honestly couldn't," Georgia said. "I'm only fourteen. I don't vote. I don't pay taxes."

"But according to you, it's your freedom that's being threatened," I reminded her.

"That's a separate issue," Robin said. "Equally important, though. The rights of children. No one ever remembers how often *they* are affected by what grownups do."

"Well, you're over eighteen," I told him. "Why didn't *you* stand up and let them have it if you're so certain about all this?"

Robin shrugged. "I wasn't prepared," he admitted. "I mean, Georgia told me what was going on, and it sounded as rotten to me as to her. But I wanted to hear it all for myself, and have a little time to think about it. I'm not crazy about shooting from the hip."

My father cleared his throat. We all looked in his direction. (You would, too, and probably do, when the same sound comes from *your* father's larynx.)

"I think Robin's right to be cautious," he announced quietly. "It wouldn't be a bad idea, Georgia, if you took a leaf from your brother's book."

"What's that supposed to mean?" she demanded.

"Just that a little patience now might avert a lot of

unpleasantness later," Father explained. "You got Robin down here, away from his studies, and undoubtedly you feel justified now that he agrees with you that Brady may be overstepping his prerogatives. I just think that before you go off enlisting the aid of your librarian and your friends and whomever, you should try to look ahead and see where all this is leading."

"It's leading to a fight, Dad," Robin said. "Either that, or to outright censorship if no one cares enough to mobilize and stand up to him."

"Wouldn't it be wiser, though," said Mother, "to wait and see what Mr. Sopwith says? I mean, just suppose he agrees with *you*."

"Fat chance," Robin judged. "After all, it was Brady who selected old Stanley."

"And Brady who can replace him if he does," Georgia said sharply.

I heard the sound of a car pulling up at the curb outside and excused myself from the table. I stopped at the front hall closet to grab a sweater, September being warm to be sure but susceptible to sudden chills. Leaving the sound of argument behind, or, more politely, family discussion, it occurred to me that if all was well and God was in His world, I wouldn't need the sweater at all.

# 4.

It wasn't until I was settled in Martin's front seat that I remembered the little pantomine in the school hallway. I was tempted to try to explain what had been going on—nothing—but then I decided that since nothing *had* happened, there was nothing to apologize for. Still, I was the slightest bit uneasy. I didn't want a confrontation. I just wanted Martin to be Martin.

The important facts are these. Martin is a senior, too. He's blond and about six feet tall, with an almost translucent complexion and startlingly clear blue eyes. Like the rest of his peers, Martin works out with weights. Ostensibly this is to give him greater power and strength on the football field, or for track. I think it's a male bonding thing: guys like to imagine themselves as tough and muscular and ready to handle anything. You'll find, usually, that the guys who do work out also hang around together. I'm not saying this is abnormal in any way; actually, it makes me smile. With all those muscles, how strange that they have to run in a pack for safety.

Anyway, the thing that makes Martin different from his cohorts is that he's very bright and not at all afraid to be sentimental, for which I'm grateful. I mean, you need a little mushiness when you're our age, like remembering the date of your first meeting, remembering each other's birthday, remembering how long you've been going together. Not that Martin and I were betrothed, or even going steady. We had simply reached a wonderful point in life where we were *together,* and people accepted us as a team. *Most* people, Darryl von Vrock apart.

Another important fact is that Martin drives a Chevrolet El Camino, pearl gray, with white sidewalls and a gun rack in its cab. There is no rifle hanging there; there is an umbrella. In the Brady household, everyone but Martin's younger brother Matthew, who is, after all, only fifteen, has a car. In ours, Mother has one (the station wagon) and so does Rick, a jalopy he paid for by working summers on road gangs, and drives to and from Northwestern. Of course, it helps that Owanka's the sort of town where it's still possible to get around on foot. Or, if Mother has a particularly frantic day and the weather is dismal, she can drop Daddy off at his store and arrange to pick him up later at five-thirty.

Moving on then, Martin and I were parked out near Mill Pond, about four miles from town, sitting in his pickup. If you must know, we kissed occasionally, and I allowed him one or two other very small, insignificant liberties that to him seemed reassurance of some future heavenly consummation devoutly wished. Anyway, after a moment to rearrange, we faced each other.

"What was all that about at your locker today?" Martin asked.

I knew, of course, what he meant. "What do you mean?" I said.

"Von Vrock," Martin answered. "He's a bird dog."

I smiled. "He thinks you have good taste," I said. "I agreed. And that was that."

"Sure?"

"Absolutely." Thank goodness it was dark. "You know," I said then, moving swiftly ahead, "your dad's upset a lot of people."

"Over what?"

"This book business."

*"The Grapes of Wrath?"*

I nodded. "To some people, what he's trying to do seems like censorship."

"It is," Martin replied simply. "I agree. I've told him so, too."

"You have?"

Martin nodded. Inwardly, I sighed. "Not that it did much good," he admitted. "Ther is more at stake here, he says, than just one book."

"Like his Council seat?"

Martin laughed. "You're wicked. And also right. Re-election just isn't automatic, you know."

"Do you think he'll get his way?"

"Probably," Martin said unenthusiastically. "Dad doesn't like to lose. At anything."

"I'll bet Matthew feels used."

"He should. It was his room that was invaded, his privacy. Dad had no right to go nosing around in there."

"Yeah, but every parent does it sooner or later. Usually they're looking for other stuff, though."

"I'll tell you, Ave, if Dad had to come across something in Matt's room, I'm glad it was just a book. Can you imagine the hellfire and damnation if he found pot or something?"

I smiled weakly. "Still and all," I said, "did *you* think the book was so terrible?"

Martin grinned. "Nope," he said. "I didn't. I liked it. It was a little long-winded, but mostly I liked it. I liked the preacher. I liked Grandpa. I felt sorry for them."

"What about the women?" I asked. "What about the people who survived and lived to see California?"

"It's easier to feel sad for people who didn't survive, I guess. The fact that they died makes them stick in your mind better."

"That's macabre," I told him.

"But true just the same," Martin answered. "How did you feel about it?"

"The book, or the survivors?"

"Both."

"I thought the book was sad and sweet in a strange way, and that it said something important about the little guys versus the big ones."

"Which brings us back to my esteemed father," Martin said.

"Except, in this case, the little guy is my sister, Georgia."

"Georgia? She's just a kid."

"She's growing."

Martin laughed. "Not fast enough to suit her, I'll bet."

"It's her brain I'm talking about, Martin. I get a funny feeling Georgia's going to cause a lot of trouble before she's through with this."

"With what exactly?"

"She's going to fight your father," I said, knowing how silly that sounded.

Martin, bless him, did not laugh then. "That doesn't sound like a very fair match," he allowed.

"Don't be too sure," I cautioned. "She's already begun to organize. She's been to Miss McCandless, the librarian. Apparently McCandless knows how to fight movements like this."

"I wouldn't call what Dad's doing a movement," Martin said. "That's too dignified. He's just looking to win his seat again, that's all."

"Maybe, but that's not what it looks like to other people."

"Like who?"

"Well, my brother Robin, for one."

Martin sat silently a moment. He likes both Robin and Rick. I guess he was surprised.

Then, after a moment more, he smiled. He reached out across the front seat and started to pull me toward him. "You know, Ave, the election's going to be here and gone so fast. Really. If I thought my father was truly serious about cleaning up the books we read, I'd fight, too. But I just can't convince myself he cares about that as much as he does the other."

"You're missing my point, sweetie pie," I said then. "No matter what your father thinks he's doing, it's what other people perceive that's going to count in the long run. And this all just might get good and bloody."

"You exaggerate. Kiss me."

"I do not. And here."

# 5.

The next morning I woke hours earlier than I wanted. I lay in bed a moment, hearing muffled voices and footsteps on the stairway. It was still shadowy out, not light yet but close enough so that, peering through my curtains, the front yard and the street seemed pewter-colored.

I slipped out of bed and into my robe and started downstairs. Robin was in the kitchen, making coffee.

"What time's your bus?" I asked, leaning against the doorframe, still bleary-eyed.

"Half an hour," he replied. "Want some coffee?"

I shook my head. "It's too adult for me," I said. "Besides, I hate its taste."

"Just as well. Want some orange juice?"

I moved into the kitchen and sat at the small table there, content to let Robin get the juice from the refrigerator and pour. He went back to the stove and poured hot water into a mug of instant coffee and then returned to sit opposite me. He sipped and then smiled a little crazily, I thought. "You know," he said, "you really haven't got any excuses."

"For what?"

"For not going to the next Council meeting."

I sighed. "Robin, give me a break. I can't go off on every goose chase Georgia dreams up."

"She's not dreaming," he said.

"Come on!" I argued. "This is not such a big deal. A man wants to get elected to a position. He finds an issue. As soon as the election is over, the whole thing will be forgotten. Over and out."

"That's too simple," Robin judged. "And also wrong. Stop and think what all this means."

"I've already done that," I said quickly. "I've talked it over with Martin. Even he agrees that his father's just running scared."

Robin shook his head. "Believe me, if you'd only look a little harder, squint, you'd see what's coming down the pike."

"I can't."

"That's why I'm glad you're up."

I was unimpressed.

"A couple of things can happen here," Robin went on. "One would be that no one bothered to come to the town Council meetings. A motion is offered, carried and passed, and a book is removed from school. A few feathers are ruffled but really too late, only after the *Herald* reports."

"What else?"

"What else is what I hope happens," Robin said. "Not for the fight, the fun. But because it really matters what happens now. There are principles involved, things you don't normally think about. Like who's responsible for what kids read? Teachers, parents, the kids? And what about the rights of kids? Why shouldn't they be allowed to read what interests them, when everyone's always screaming about poor reading scores to begin with?"

"Wait a minute," I tried to break in. Unsuccessfully.

"And if Brady's committee comes up with a lot of

do's and don'ts for other books," Robin continued, "what about the freedom of a teacher to do his or her job as best he can? What about freedom of religion, if it comes to that? If Brady's crew makes a call based on references to God or the devil or whatever, aren't they really forcing the rest of us to see the world through their eyes?"

"Hold it!" I finally cautioned. "I'm not saying those things don't count, Robin. But there's just one question you have to answer for me and I don't think you can do it. Suppose *The Grapes of Wrath* wasn't assigned reading. Do you honestly think kids our age would want to read it? Of their own free will, their own choice?"

Robin grinned. "That's a good question," he admitted. "And I can't answer it, you're right. But what matters more is the freedom of choice. *If* they want to."

"And what about freedom of choice for these kids' parents?" I asked then. "Don't they have the right to come down hard if they feel their kids are being exposed to stuff they can't approve?"

"You assume that parents even know what's going on," Robin countered.

"They certainly will if your vision of the future holds," I said firmly. "If you make something of all this—you and Georgia—you can bet your bottom dollar that parents are going to go through the roof, take sides, get involved."

Robin smiled. "For every set of parents who favor Mr. Brady's proposal, there will be one who oppose it."

I tapped my finger against the side of my glass. "What is it you really want, Robin? I mean, for all intents and purposes, you don't even live here any more."

"What I want is not to see censorship slip into Owanka unnoticed," he replied. "If we have to have it, I want it openly understood. I want people aware of

what it means, how far it can go. I want people to fight
for it, if they want, or to fight against it. I want people
informed."

"But that's the job the *Herald* is doing," I objected.
"Whose fault is it if no one reads the damned thing?"

Robin shrugged. "No one's," he admitted. "That's just
life. But it doesn't have to be. You're sitting on top of
a fairly powerful little rag yourself."

"*The Hawk?*"

"What else?" Robin smiled. "It wouldn't surprise me
if more parents snuck a look at that paper than read
the *Herald*."

"You have a fairly low opinion of adults, it seems to
me."

"On the contrary," he said. "I have a fairly exalted
opinion of Georgia, and of what you can do to help her."

"You're going to make an awesome lawyer," I as-
sessed, not unpleasantly.

"I know. Now, say you'll go."

"I'll go." I was going to add something but I stopped.

"But you're not happy," Robin concluded for me.

"The very words."

"Just do me one favor," Robin asked.

"One more," I corrected.

"One more, then," and he smiled. "Don't try to walk
a thin line. Don't try to make sense of both sides. Don't
balance what you hear with what you imagine, or even
with what you feel, if it comes to that. Just report what
goes on, who says what, on which side people stand.
What's at stake. Let your readers draw their own conclusions."

"Even if they're not the ones you want them to
draw?" I asked shrewdly.

"Even then," Robin returned soberly. "All I'm asking

is that you try to be an impartial journalist. Report the news. Trust your public."

"You know, Robin, sometimes you are astonishingly naïve."

"Or incredibly clever," he amended, winking at me. "Now, I've got to get out of here or I'll miss the bus." He stood up and quickly kissed the top of my head. "See you."

I nodded. "So long."

I heard the front door close and heard him running along the sidewalk toward town and the bus stop.

It occurred to me then that Georgia had called upon Robin when she felt in need. And I knew I would, too. Suddenly, I realized that people seemed to expect him to handle problems, answer questions, give fair advice, help out in a bind. I wondered who for Robin provided the same human services.

# 6.

The settlers who planned Owanka had an eye for natural beauty. A freshwater pond was discovered and Owanka built on its banks. On the east side of the pond is an old-fashioned town square, surrounded even today by brick buildings no more than three stories tall, some of which have white Colonial columns on their porches, some of which have shutters at their windows. There are still shingles, if you can believe it, announcing a lawyer's or a doctor's office. There is a department store (Younkers) on the north side of the square and City Drug stands to one side of this (around the corner from my Dad's hardware store) and Chez Elle, the tiny boutique where I work on Saturdays, to the other.

Along the west side of the square is a park that leads down to the banks of our now algae-covered pond, with benches and shuffleboard courts, and a playground with slides, jungle gym, swings, and sandpiles. Not a lot happens there any more. As a matter of fact, to the city fathers, too little happens along the square at all. The problem reputedly is that there is also, out east of town a couple of miles, a new shopping mall with a sports shop, a record and card store, a Sears, a discount drug, a pizza joint, a Sizzler's Steakhouse, a supermarket, and a bookstore. Since Owanka High is about halfway between "downtown" and this relative paradise, you can imagine where a lot of kids hang out.

On the south side of the square is the town hall, which is a multipurpose building that includes the courthouse, the local jail, a Department of Motor Vehicles office, a game warden's office, and so on. The building itself is not unimpressive, having columns freshly painted each spring, running up the full three-story height, and an equally imposing set of steps leading up to it. There is a statue at the top of these, dedicated to and depicting one Major General Leonard Carl Padway, our very own Civil War hero who, despite the fact that his troops were on the run and scattered across the Pennsylvania countryside at Gettysburg, nonetheless held single-handedly a bumpy, insignificant but somehow immortal ridge against the CSA crowd.

I didn't tell anyone I was going to attend the next meeting of the City Council. I didn't want to be laughed at by my friends, and I certainly didn't want Georgia shooting me an "I knew you would" across the dinner table. I had promised Robin I would go and so I went. I took the precaution of borrowing Martin Brady's cassette recorder, in case I developed writer's cramp or the action became too fast and furious for me to get down accurately. The meeting was to begin at three-thirty and I arrived in the courtroom where these friendly get-togethers are held just a few minutes before that.

I took a seat near the back of the room and scanned the dais. A few of our town's more notable citizens were already in place, talking among themselves, including Fairchild Brady, all dressed in a cleanly pressed white shirt and a pin-striped suit with Oxford shoes, his gray-white hair slicked back and just the slightest bit damp over his red forehead. I put my purse down on the floor near my feet and as I straightened, someone's nearby cough came to my ears and I turned in that direction. To say I was surprised is an understatement.

It was Martin Brady, *my* Martin, who had sent a throaty greeting! Worse, he was seated next to my gangling sister Georgia!

On Georgia's other side was our school librarian, Miss McCandless—about thirty-two or -three, tall but with a nice figure, always well dressed—this afternoon in a gray flannel suit and simple blouse, her hair hanging loose and free, a light brown. She has deep brown eyes that seem extraordinarily trusting, though it may be they seem so since they're magnified by clear plastic glasses. I had only spoken with Miss McCandless a few times in the past three years, and I say here, truly, that I had feelings neither for nor against her. She's always been cordial to me and helpful on those occasions that required it. She's never tried to make a reader of me (she never had to; my mother, Alva McCormick Van Buren, did that) and she never tried to push my reading in any particular direction that *she* thought valuable or progressive.

I waved weakly at Martin, wondering how on earth Georgia managed to get him to come. I was a little angry, in fact, that Martin had not told me he was coming, giving me his recorder without asking questions or volunteering answers.

The meeting did not begin promptly. I organized my machine and my notebook and continued to look around. There were a few friends of my parents, people whose names I knew or whose children I went to school with. Owanka's single good trial lawyer sat in my pew, a few feet away. There were two people from the *Herald,* a photographer who sat in the front row, ready, I assumed, to snap any scene of fireworks that erupted; a reporter who took a seat just behind Georgia and Miss McCandless whom I vaguely recognized as Susan Woods. She was not very old, twenty-one or so, obviously on the *Herald* in order to start her underpaid

career, aching no doubt for her Big Break, the chance
to move on to the *Chicago Tribune* or the *St. Louis Post-
Dispatch,* not to mention the *Des Moines Register and
Tribune.*

At about ten minutes to four, Mr. Brady finally
raised his gavel and called for order. The Widow Clarke
was directed to read the minutes of the last meeting,
but then, in the same breath, unless there were objections, Mr. Brady called for the minutes to be accepted
without being read, and all heads at the table nodded
agreement except for Mrs. Clarke's. Clearly she did not
appreciate having her duty ignored. (Mrs. Clarke, a
woman nearly fifty, has maneuvered her way through
life on the arms of three—count 'em, three!—successive
husbands. In a town our size, that is no mean feat,
*finding* the talent, not to mention marrying it. Each
man—first Regis, then Beckmann, and finally Clarke—
succumbed to disease each swiftly and in theory without undue pain. Naturally enough, among the younger
crowd, this gave rise to speculation about Mrs. Clarke's
culinary skills.)

There followed some discussion of vandalism on the
square, in particular relation to the newly installed
parking meters there, which meant a loss of revenue to
the city. Before long, though, Mr. Brady edged the meeting around to what was on his own mind—the report of
the provisional committee on suitable literature in
Owanka High School.

Stanley Sopwith stood in place and held a sheaf of
paper with visible ink notations. There was no mention
of other committee members or names of alternates.
Mr. Sopwith cleared his throat.

"On Tuesday last, the eighteenth of September,
1980, a provisional committee was appointed to investigate whether books assigned the schoolchildren of
Owanka Senior High School, Owanka, Iowa, were suit-

able to those same children in terms of values, morals, language, and imagery."

Mr. Sopwith stopped to examine the crowd in the courtroom a second before continuing. "Mr. Stanley Sopwith was appointed chairman and endeavored as directed to examine in particular a novel entitled *The Grapes of Wrath,* published in 1939, written by Mr. John Steinbeck, and awarded the Pulitzer Prize for that year."

I had forgotten that about the book and was surprised—astonished, really, when I thought about it—that the Council would even begin to take on this project. I mean, short of the Nobel, what bigger prize is there?

I waited patiently, my tape recorder humming discreetly in my lap, for Mr. Sopwith to continue. I looked up at him and found him looking directly down at me. (Mr. Sopwith looks exactly like the famous old Sopwith Flying Camel, the airplane Snoopy guides as he relentlessly searches the skies for the infamous Red Baron. A grain merchant and construction company vice-president, Stanley Sopwith is wifeless, childless, humorless, with ears that stick out so you can almost picture the two-wing construction of the old plane. His face is gray, his figure sparse, his clothing pressed so often you can see the shine of serge under certain lights.)

"I think it might be best," Stanley Sopwith announced then, "if women and whatever young people there are in the room leave the hall temporarily until I conclude my report."

No one moved.

"I'm serious," Stanley Sopwith insisted. "This gets pretty rough."

"Stanley?" It was Mrs. Clarke. "Really, dear, I think most of us are adult enough, and discreet enough, to be able to take what you're going to tell us in the spirit in which it is offered. Do, go ahead."

Stanley Sopwith was not happy. He waited another moment, looking out at us all with his eyebrows raised. Finally, he gave a regretful nod and cleared his throat once more. I suspected he was less angry that we were staying than he was at what he was about to read from the papers in his hands.

"I myself have not yet concluded reading the book in question," he began. He looked directly out at his audience, almost challengingly, unashamed. He departed from his prepared text. "I couldn't!" he announced loudly. "It was too much! I never in my life ran across anything like it!"

At this there was a slight stir in the room.

"Stanley," Mr. Brady cautioned, "try to be impartial, if you please."

"That's impossible!" Stanley Sopwith shot back. "Why, if I'd ever known this book was in our school, I'd have single-handedly raided that place and torn it out, every last copy, book by book!"

"What does your report conclude?" asked Mr. Brady quietly.

Stanley Sopwith managed to calm himself, marginally. "In my initial perusal," he said, reading again from his report but looking up every few seconds as he continued, "I found blasphemy, un-Americanism, the espousal of communism and other foreign ideologies, not to mention more examples of obscene language than I had ever before heard or read."

We were spellbound, breathless, waiting. Sopwith smiled then, nodding to himself, as if to say *I warned you and you wouldn't leave so you have only yourselves to blame.*

"In the first one hundred pages," Mr. Sopwith went

on at last, "this is what I found. And mind you, this is only the first hundred pages!

"There are twenty uses of the word 'damn.' There are thirty-one instances of the word 'hell.' 'Goddamn' is used fifteen times. 'Jesus' eighteen, 'Christ' seven, and 'son of a bitch' twelve."

He paused, triumphant, eyes aglitter. He half-turned toward Mr. Brady, expecting I suppose to be told that he need go no further. Mr. Brady said nothing, just sat motionless, a tiny smile on his lips, coaxing silently. Mr. Sopwith waited a second more and then turned back toward the courtroom.

"The word 'bastard' is used eight times. Drinking, or being drunk, is mentioned approvingly nine times. God's name is taken twenty-five times!"

One could almost sense that Mr. Sopwith had begun to feel he was on a winning roll. His voice got stronger and speeded up, and he read from his list with increasing anger and mounting pleasure.

"Fornicating with women is mentioned approvingly eight times, as in 'tom-cattin' and 'layin' with.' Killing, and showing no signs of remorse, killing human beings is mentioned four times, along with an avowed intention to do the same again, guiltlessly. Rape is mentioned twice. The word 'bitch' is used four times. 'Ass' is used three. The lack of differentiation between good and evil, between sin and goodness, virtue and its lack, is mentioned three times. Euphemisms for the male member are used four times. And the following are mentioned at least once, all in these same one hundred pages: 'breasts,' 'crap,' 'orgasm,' 'cussing,' 'screwing,' 'testicles.' There is one instance of a pig eating a human child! And there is one instance of people actually having sex...with animals!"

I can only say how grateful I was to have Martin's

tape recorder. I could never have kept up with Mr. Sopwith's shopping list.

"All in all," Mr. Sopwith wound down, "I found two hundred and seventeen instances of what I consider objectionable language, imagery, or ideology. That is more than two instances per page, and certainly more than any book ought rightfully to have in its entirety."

Mr. Sopwith was perspiring and weaving just the slightest bit in his place.

"Thank you, Stanley," Mr. Brady said comfortingly. "That was quite a task and we're grateful to you for doing it so well."

Mr. Sopwith barely smiled and looked around, apparently wondering whether he was to resume his seat or remain standing, half-expecting applause, perhaps. Mr. Brady stood up then himself, taking the weight of decision from Sopwith's shoulders, and Stanley sank into his chair, exhausted but happy.

But standing, too, was Martin Brady, waiting to be recognized by his father. I held my breath.

"Yes, Martin?" said Mr. Brady.

"I guess a lot of people, hearing Mr. Sopwith's report, would be shocked," Martin said carefully. "But I have one question for him I'd like answered."

"And what is that?" asked his father.

"Could Mr. Sopwith please tell us what the book is about?"

There were one or two moderately well-camouflaged sniggers from behind me. I did not turn around.

Mr. Brady turned to Stanley Sopwith. "Stanley?"

Mr. Sopwith rose to his feet again. "You mean the story?"

Martin Brady nodded that that was what he meant.

Mr. Sopwith reddened. "I could not," he said defiantly. "And I wouldn't, even if I could. It was all I could do to get through one hundred pages of that filth!

Who cares what kind of story the man thinks he's telling?"

"Well, sir," Martin said courteously, "I think that may matter to some of us here. You see, I read that book in tenth grade myself. I don't feel sullied by it, or cheapened, or cynical."

"Probably weren't so goddamned pure to begin with," Mr. Sopwith said under his breath. Mr. Brady turned quickly to glare at him.

"You see, I'm not certain," Martin went on quietly, "that anyone could have told the same kind of tragic story Mr. Steinbeck did without using most of the words and ideas you found so threatening."

Martin sat down then, not smirking, just finished with what he had to say.

"You stick to your guns, son!" came an angry shout from the back corner of the courtroom. We all turned to see a man of at least eighty-five standing, red in the face, hand in the air made into a fist.

"Mr. Nagle, I believe?" said Mr. Brady, ever the observant chairman.

"You believe right, Fairchild Brady," Mr. Nagle announced. "I was principal of that school, you know, when that book first came out. I taught it in my English classes. I was the one who put it on a reading list for the first time. It's a story we older people know about because we lived it, we saw people broken by it. It's an honest and heartbreaking job, that book, and the language it uses is the language of its time and place."

Mr. Brady nodded placatingly and attempted to cut off Mr. Nagle in mid-sentence. "Then you think the book is suit—"

"Damned right I do!" said Mr. Nagle. "There isn't another book about the Depression that even begins to touch it. It's American and solid and true. And if a bunch of right-wing ignoramuses try to remove it from the hands of young people who should *know* about that part of their country's history, well, I for one will go to the wall defending it."

"Now, just a minute," Stanley Sopwith said, standing and pointing his finger at Mr. Nagle. A flashbulb erupted.

"If the shoe fits, Sopwith," Mr. Nagle challenged.

"I'm no ignoramus!" shouted Sopwith.

"No, you just read a hundred pages of one of America's greatest books without the faintest idea of what the man was saying. That's not ignorance. That's illiteracy!"

"Gentlemen, gentlemen," cautioned Mr. Brady, "there's no need to—"

"Yes, there is too, Fairchild," shouted Nagle. "You've got to call a spade a spade, no matter what. There's more than enough to attend to in this town without meddling in the education of the young."

"We're hardly meddling, Benjamin," Mr. Brady said smoothly. "All we're doing is questioning the good sense of a teacher assigning something to his or her class that we feel is lurid and cheap or pornographic."

"Pornographic!" snorted Mr. Nagle, still on his feet. "I'll tell you what's pornographic! Censorship, that's what!"

At that point, the photographer from the *Herald* sprang up from his seat and swung around quickly to flash a picture of Mr. Nagle, hand raised, the cords in his neck clear, his eyes wide in outrage.

There was a little commotion then, as spectators talked among themselves and began to argue.

"Ladies and gentlemen, please, please," called Fairchild Brady, both of *his* hands spread wide at shoulder height pacifically.

After a few seconds the confusion lessened and the

room quieted once more. Mr. Brady was gratified and smiled out at us all.

"The reason we're here this afternoon is to hear Stanley's report, and to make a recommendation whether or not the suitability of this particular book should be placed before the community at large. We've heard opposing points of view. Are any others prepared to speak for or against?"

People looked around, nudged one another, coughed nervously, and waited. Then Miss McCandless rose in her place. "Yes, ma'am." Mr. Brady recognized her.

"Without taking sides in this issue, I'd like to introduce myself," Miss McCandless said quietly, soothingly. "I'm librarian at Owanka High and my name is Laura McCandless. It might be helpful, whether or not you eventually put this issue before the voters, to tell you that at the library we have forms that can be used to make these matters a little clearer." She turned to pick up her purse and to begin edging her way out of her spot between Martin and Georgia, walking toward the front of the room. She was carrying white paper sheets with mimeographed writing on them. She offered one of these to Mr. Brady, and the rest she handed up and over the table to Mrs. George Nichols, the chairperson of the School Board Committee.

(Mrs. Nichols, mother of four, PTA Parent of the Year, stalwart of the First Baptist Church, winner of two blue ribbons at the Iowa State Fair for her strawberry-rhubarb pies, as well as a director of the Owanka Public Library, is about forty-five, very trim, with a nice, thoughtful smile and probably not an unkind bone in her body. Her most striking physical feature is her nose, which is as pure and straight and photogenic a structure as I've ever seen, and I am positively covetous. She is also, because of the way our town operates, nominal chairperson of the School Board. Owanka has only two elementary schools, one junior high and one senior high, which gives its educational establishment a rare unity. There are seldom arguments about school taxes or improvements in teachers' salaries. Everyone seems to agree—or did, until last fall—that young people should be properly educated and successful and productive citizens. Also that the best teachers of children are *teachers*, professionals hired and trained and performing efficiently at their selected task. It's very businesslike.)

"I brought these along," Miss McCandless explained, "because from time to time other complaints are made about particular books in our collection, and these help to identify not just the books, but the precise reasons why someone feels they are unsuitable for young people."

Mr. Brady looked down at the piece of paper in his hand and scanned it quickly, handing it then behind him to Stanley Sopwith. Then he smiled rather oilily at Miss McCandless and his voice became slippery. "I can see how helpful these might be in another case," he said. "But in this instance, we have already identified the book and the reasons we think it unworthy of our younger citizens' time and attention."

"I'm not so certain of that," Mrs. Nichols said suddenly, startling Mr. Brady, who turned toward her with a frown. "Really, Fairchild, this is a very sensible idea."

"I don't doubt that," Mr. Brady assured her. "But it seems to me that perhaps in other instances, after we've taken care of this book, we can—"

"No, I think this is the perfect time," Mrs. Nichols persisted. "I think, for example, that if Stanley would fill out one of these, then the School Board would have a record of his complaint and *we* could act on it without going to all the trouble and expense and clearly the argument of a public hearing. After all, that's what the School Board Committee is for, Fairchild."

Mr. Brady scowled. "Just how would you go about weighing the complaint then, Louise?" he asked.

"Well," said Mrs. Nichols thoughtfully, "I would imagine that when we received one of these, from whomever it might be and about whatever book, we would examine the book ourselves and come to a reasonable conclusion about its merits and value. You know, Fairchild, our responsibility is to the young people of Owanka, not to the adults around them."

"And just what about the adults?" Stanley Sopwith asked angrily. "Shouldn't we, based on our experience of the world, be able to make some of those decisions that help young people get on in the world?"

"Of course you should, Stanley," said Mrs. Nichols logically, gently. "And you are especially free to do so with your own children."

That was a groovy, but low, blow, because old Stanley has no kids.

"What *is* on that piece of paper?" asked Mrs. Clarke.

Mr. Brady retrieved his copy from Stanley Sopwith and spoke directly to her. "There are simple questions," he explained. "She wants to know the name of the book and its author. The reason one might find it objectionable. What the book is about. What other book one would recommend that covers the same subject that is more suitable. Whether one read all the book, parts of it, scanned it, heard about it. What grades your children are in."

"Well," Mrs. Clarke leaned back in her chair, her snow-white bosom bouncing ever so slightly, "I think that all sounds perfectly reasonable. Why *don't* we let the School Board Committee deal with this?"

"Because they'll duck it!" Stanley Sopwith said

hotly. "We go with this kind of thing, and it's the last we'll ever hear."

"I take exception to that, Mister Sopwith," said Mrs. Nichols with some annoyance. "What this would institute is a channel for complaints and a system for dealing with them."

"But what we have here is a particular case," Mr. Brady said rather grandly, "not something to be handled in the future. And Mr. Sopwith was directed to give his recommendations, not his literary opinion, which he has done. The only question that stands before the Council now is whether we feel strongly enough to put the issue to our fellow townspeople for them to judge themselves."

"But surely, Fairchild, when Miss McCandless has brought us this—?" said Mrs. Nichols urgently. "I mean, you can see how heated people get, how angry. Surely this would be a perfect way of examining and weighing the merits of a book without making people purple in the face."

"I agree entirely," said Mr. Brady easily, "for the future, Louise. For the future. But we have a book here and now before us that requires our attention."

"Vote!" said Amos Allen suddenly and gruffly. We all heard him speak but when we looked at him it appeared as though he were still motionless in his chair. Amos is a widower, glum and drear, but nonetheless fodder, one supposes, for Widow Clarke—never say die! He's lived alone for years, out on a farm just beyond the city limits, although thirty acres of it or so are incorporated. He has no help there, working and farming alone and, rumor hath it, making a considerable amount of money from cattle, hogs, and soybeans. We *think* he and his wife had a son but no one seems to recall ever meeting the boy. Mr. Allen says little, nods sometimes, seems frequently to doze in church (Lutheran, our own, which is how I know) or in public. He's narrow where Mr. Brady is rotund; his skin is weathered white, summer and winter, from the ever-present hat on his head, and yet his hair is startlingly dark and full.

"I second the motion!" Stanley Sopwith declared next.

Mr. Brady smiled paternally. "The motion is called. All in favor?" He looked down the line of the Council table. Every hand but Mr. Hubbell's, the mayor, and Mrs. Nichols' was raised. "The motion is carried, then," Mr. Brady said happily. "Stanley, would you like to place the question?"

Mr. Sopwith stood at his place as though ordered to jump. Miss McCandless made her way tactfully back to her own seat. There was silence in the high-ceilinged room.

"Well," Stanley Sopwith began, "I guess the question is whether a separate ballot should be printed and distributed along with the regular one, this one asking whether people think that book, *The Grapes of Wrath*, should be removed from the curriculum of the tenth grade at Owanka High, and from the library there."

"The library?" Miss McCandless was heard to gasp.

"Might as well," Stanley said, glaring down at her harshly.

"All right, now, folks," Mr. Brady said, once more in charge, "you've heard the question put. Now, let's vote."

"Who's going to pay for the ballots?" asked Mr. Allen glumly, his mouth barely moving.

"Well, Amos, I imagine we can find a little extra money in the budget somehow," Mr. Brady assured him. "We're not talking about thousands of dollars, are we? Probably only fifty or sixty bucks all tolled."

Mr. Allen nodded, apparently satisfied.

"Now then," Mr. Brady continued, "all in favor of Mr. Sopwith's motion?"

We all watched closely. Mr. Hubbell did not move, since a mayor had no vote. Stanley Sopwith's hand shot up toward the ceiling instantly. Mr. Brady's hand was lifted almost beneficently, as a Pope's would be. Mrs. Clarke—after years of being deferential to three heads-of-household, and those habits are hard to break—hesitated a minute and then smiled at Mr. Brady as her own hand was raised.

Mrs. Nichols sat without moving, her hands clasped together in her lap.

Mr. Allen frowned and twitched momentarily but his hand did not climb into view. Instead, he looked at Fairchild Brady and said, almost under his breath, "We shouldn't be getting involved in this."

Mr. Brady seemed not to hear him. He turned around in a semicircle, pleased as a proud parent, congratulating himself and his cohorts silently. "Well then, I guess the motion is carried," he announced.

"Fairchild Brady!" It was Mr. Nagle at the back of the room, standing once more, his face flushed. Mr. Brady turned. "Do you have some new piece of business, Mr. Nagle?"

"I surely do," returned Mr. Nagle positively. "If you think you can ramrod that book into a cannon and shoot it out of existence, you're dead wrong! You've got a fight on your hands!"

"The electorate will have its chance to decide, Benjamin," Mr. Brady said smoothly. "Surely, when all is said and done, that's the best way to handle things in a democracy like ours."

"I'm not so all-fired sure that your kind of democracy is like mine!" Mr. Nagle answered angrily, turning then and elbowing his way toward the double doors of the courtroom.

"Well, we'll see, won't we?" Mr. Brady asked quietly.

"You're damned right we'll see!" Mr. Nagle shot back just before he pushed open the doors to disappear into the hallway.

# 7.

There wasn't much official business left to transact and the Council meeting was adjourned fairly rapidly. I stood up to gather my things, determined to slip away quietly without facing up to Martin and perhaps exploding. I felt betrayed that his mind should so easily have been made up while mine was still somewhere suspended uneasily, waiting. *The Hawk* would get the benefit of an eyewitness account of the day's proceedings, not only because the school was involved, but also since one of its staff had stepped forward to make a small public gesture of peace-seeking. Actually, of avoidance. Miss McCandless must have suspected how people could get unhinged by something like this. I certainly never did.

The biggest difficulty I faced just then was writing the article in time to make the 8 A.M. deadline for *The Hawk* in the morning. We go to press a full twenty-four hours before the paper makes its appearance in school hallways. I didn't have a lot of leeway.

Someone took hold of my elbow and I turned, half-expecting it would be Martin, his pink, dreamy face smiling down at me. It was. "Come on, Ava, I'll drive you home."

"Don't you have the wrong Van Buren?" I asked a little snottily. "Doesn't Georgia need a lift?"

Martin laughed softly. "No," he answered, his hand still on my arm, guiding me down the steps of the courthouse, "she has some secret meeting to attend. You know your sister."

"That's precisely why I asked," I said. "Why didn't you go with her, since you two are suddenly so thick?"

"Because, Ava, I'd rather spend the time with you."

It's difficult to argue with sincerity. "Well," I allowed, "you can drive me back to school. If I'm going to put anything in *The Hawk,* I ought to work there, and fast."

"Good," Martin said. "I have to get back to practice, anyway," and he very gentlemanly opened the passenger door on his El Camino for me.

He slid into the driver's seat and started the car. "Now," I demanded as we pulled away from the square, "how did Georgia con you into going to the meeting?"

"She didn't con me, exactly," Martin said. "She needed a ride and happened to run into me in the halls. After all, she is *your* sister, Ave. What could I do?"

"Nuts!" I was unconvinced. "You didn't have to stay."

"No, I didn't," Martin said seriously, staring out the windshield as he drove. "But in a way, I had to. I'd made up my mind, in advance, mind you, not always such a hot thing to do. But as it turned out, I was right."

"About what?"

"About how the meeting would end up," he said. "I haven't told Dad this, but I don't think I want to be around very much in the next few weeks."

"What does *that* mean?"

"I think I'll go spend time at Barney Ellis' house."

"I don't get you."

"I'm going to move in with Barney until the election's over," Martin explained. "I can't dissuade Dad, convince him he's off-base. He feels too strongly about this thing, I guess, and he does want to stay on the Council.

It would be like taking a hundred runs at a brick wall.
I'm willing, but not dumb."

"What will he say?"

Martin shrugged. "He probably won't have anything
to say. I'll just grab some stuff and move into Barney's.
If Dad blows his top, it'll be at Matthew or Mom. Too
bad, but that's better than a six-week shouting match."

I wondered at the ease of Martin's decision. "What
about the Ellises?" I asked. "How will they feel?"

"I hope they'll agree with me," Martin said. "You
know, Ave, this dumb ballot thing could be just the tip
of an iceberg. What happens later? Does the School
Board Committee, or my father, get to make up a list
of forbidden books? Books that automatically would be
removed from a class, or forbidden altogether? I mean,
suppose certain words show up in one. Does that mean
it's excluded instantly, regardless of how good or bad
a book it is? Who has the power?"

"Right now, your old man."

"Not really," Martin said. "He's making trouble, but
if enough people get together to fight him, then I think
this can be stopped."

"Are you enlisting?"

"I might," he said, looking over at me quickly.
"Wouldn't you?"

Fortunately, we were approaching good old Owanka
High.

I leaned across the cab to give Martin a quick kiss.
Then, opening my door, and knowing I was copping
out, I said, "I am a member of the working press, you
know. We don't take sides. We report, pure and simply.
Period."

# 8.

"But I'm not asking for all that much!" Georgia said sullenly to my father at dinner that night. "All I want to be able to do is pull my own weight. I mean, that's what you've always told us we had to do."

My father nodded seriously. "I still believe that," he said. "But I also believe that if you're going to get so involved in this, that it will mean more, much more to you, if you have to raise your own funds."

"What about your savings account?" asked Mother then.

"How do you think the rich get richer?" Jonny asked quickly with a sudden broad smile.

"Oh, for heaven's sakes!" Georgia said in exasperation.

"Don't you have that much saved up?" I asked.

Georgia blushed. "Sure, I guess I do," she admitted, turning to give me a patented, melted-butter smile. "But that's supposed to be for college."

"See?" Jonny crowed and started to laugh. So did we all.

"This isn't funny!" Georgia complained, her smile disappearing. "Look at it this way. I'd be the representative of the Van Buren family. I mean, suppose everyone chipped in! I'm certainly not proud."

"Who else is involved?" asked Mother then. "I mean, everything seems to have happened so quickly."

"Well," Georgia began, smiling once more, now serenely, "there's me. And Miss McCandless, of course, although her participation's supposed to be secret, undercover, if you know what I mean. And Mr. Nagle, who used to teach English and was actually principal years and years ago. And there's Mrs. Nichols. Oh, and Mr. Barton, who lives around the corner. He's your friend, Dad. You go fishing in Canada with him. I talked to him on my way home."

My father nodded, apparently unsurprised that his friend's name was listed on Georgia's new committee.

"Is that all?" I asked.

"No," Georgia answered strongly. "Robin's joining, too."

"Long-distance?" asked Jonny.

"Yes," Georgia fibbed. "I know he will. And maybe even Rick."

"But you haven't solicited them yet," I guessed.

"I *will*."

"And," my mother added quietly, "Mrs. Rasmussen out at the farm."

"Alva," Father said, "I thought this was all news to you."

"It was," said Mother, nodding. "But it seems Georgia's committee, or its formation, is sweeping the countryside. She called me just before Ava got home."

Father's eyebrows raised slightly. "Anyone else we know?"

My mother nodded. "Reverend Fickett," she said.

"Really?" Father asked.

"*And* Donald Arrand," Mother announced, the weight of her words stunningly heavy.

My father sighed, troubled, but then he brightened a bit. "Well, there you are, Georgia girl. Go get Mr.

Arrand to give you a loan. Perhaps the bank will advance your dues."

Donald Arrand is president of the Owanka National Growers Bank. "I wonder," Father went on, "what those board meetings will be like for the next few weeks," he mused, remembering that Fairchild Brady was also on the board.

"You're ignoring the point," Georgia complained. "I am trying to put my money where my mouth is."

"Then you can do that on your own, sweetheart," Father said gently. "And it will mean more to you, make you feel better for having sacrificed something you're holding tightly to, sacrificed it for something in which you believe."

"Something in which *I* believe?" asked Georgia, suddenly wide-eyed. The tone and tenor of her question brought my own ears to attention.

My father's mouth turned down at the corners. "Other people may not feel quite so strongly as you do, Georgia, or agree with you."

"Are you saying you're on the other side?" she demanded.

"No, I'm not saying that," Father answered. "All I'm saying is that I'm thinking about all this, diligently. I'm rereading the book, too."

"You are?" Mother asked.

Father nodded.

"And?" coaxed my mother.

"And, I'm not sure, Alva," said Father. "One thing is for sure, there *is* an awful lot of rough language involved."

"There *is* a lot of rough language in the world," I said needlessly.

"I know there is," said Father. "But I'll tell you something. I'm not at all certain I don't agree with Fairchild Brady. Our country seems to be going downhill pell-mell. Morals aren't what they were. The crime rate is up. People are dissatisfied, too impatient to work hard for their just rewards, so they picket and burn and loot. Towns like ours are the backbone of this country, after all. Maybe if we straightened ours up a little, stood taller, made a stand, maybe we could actually begin to turn things around."

"*Very* slowly," I slipped in.

"Admittedly," Father agreed. "But also, I think, proudly."

"Fred, I am absolutely amazed at you," said Mother.

"No reason to be, Alva," said Father in return. "I said I hadn't made up my mind. I'm just leaning."

"My own father!" wailed Georgia suddenly, putting her head in her hands dramatically and moaning.

"Wait a minute," I said, trying to appease her. "There are hundreds of books you can read. Besides, if you were all so hot for this one, it seems to me you'd have already read it on the sly."

"I do not believe someone your age can be so dumb!" Georgia said, raising her head and putting the flats of her hands on the table. "You are completely missing the whole point! I may not even like the silly book, Ava," she said angrily, "but I certainly know I do not like being told I can't read it because it's bad for me. That decision is strictly up to me, I think."

"Well," said Father slowly, "not entirely, sweetheart. What are parents for, after all?"

"To give comfort and aid and support!" Georgia shot back without blinking.

Father laughed softly. "And also to see that our loved ones are cared for and treated humanely and kept from harmful things."

"A book is not harmful!" Georgia shrieked.

"*This* book might be," argued Father without raising his voice.

"It isn't," I said finally. "Really and truly, Daddy, I mean language apart. All it is is the story of one family who—"

"I know, Ava," said Father. "I'm rereading it, remember? The question is, can that story be told without those words? I rather think it can. Even that it should have been, perhaps."

"But Fred, you're asking an artist to conform to *your* rules," Mother pointed out. "You wouldn't tell a painter what colors to use, or what style would please *you* most."

"No, I wouldn't," Father defended logically. "But I might not buy the picture for my own home if I didn't like what was in it."

"But surely," Mother persisted, "you wouldn't keep someone else from buying it and hanging it in his home?"

"No, of course not," agreed Father.

"Well, there you are!" Georgia crowed happily.

"Shhh!" I hissed at her. "Let Mother say that."

And of course, Mother should have been given that chance. Because right there, right that very minute, the Van Buren family could have meshed and settled and then, when the moment came, stood firm.

It didn't.

# 9.

There were articles other than mine on the front page of *The Hawk*. There were also two pictures, one of the action during the season's first football game (a win) and one a head-and-shoulders shot of our new French teacher.

My own piece started in the lower right-hand corner (*please turn to page 4*) and its headlines, GRAPES STILL SOUR, was, I thought, apt enough to catch a few eyes. I may have been wrong. I did not hear a lot of discussion, or congratulation (which is more to the point), about it that day, or the day after. And in a way, I can understand. The sides were still being drawn up, people were making silent choices, no one seemed ready yet to take a stand and stick to it.

I tried to do what Robin had advised: report, sit back, let the reader himself decide whether or not he wanted to get involved. I didn't advocate anything in particular because I wasn't certain what to press for. Should we take to the streets over a *book?* Should we leave home, march, carry torches, raise funds, put up billboards, print handouts, wear sheets? I mean, what do you do when you're disenfranchised and other people are allowed to decide your fate?

Of course, one reason, I supposed, for the lack of

reader response was simple. Half the kids at O. High had already read the book and, as far as anyone could tell, had come through the experience unscarred. So, in the long run, why would they care? As for the other half, reading the book was not the first thing on their lists of things desperately longed for. They *would* read it, of course, as assigned, but being ordinary mortals, there were lots of other things they'd rather do.

When I read Susan Woods' piece in the *Herald* about the same meeting, I realized how little I had done and how badly. But I also understood almost at once what my article had lacked: a definite point of view. Clearly, Susan Woods knew on which side of the road she stood. One could tell simply by her selection of people to be quoted, by reading what she chose to be printed. From Miss McCandless, for example, came what seemed a very reasonable, thoughtful, and appropriate idea.

"'I've never been involved personally in anything like this before,' said Ms. McCandless after the meeting. 'But the American Library Association has been, and this approach to complaints and their value has been found useful. I doubt very much whether anyone would question the value of the book as much as its form. I'm sure teachers and librarians would be happy enough to substitute if they could find something equally distinguished.'"

Also, Susan Woods seemed to be able to take a wider view of the argument than I had. "Censorship cases such as this are not unique. Readers will recall the heated arguments and actual physical violence that took place in West Virginia a few years ago over curriculum challenges, as well as more recently on New York's Long Island and in southern California's Orange County. With the emergence of a national New Right, politically and morally, other movements have sprung up in Texas and Illinois that seek to militate personal habits and preferences."

Susan Woods' point of view was certainly clear in this last line.

Of course, one of the big differences between her piece and mine was that hers was accompanied by two pictures: one of Mr. Sopwith perspiring and gesturing, and one of Mr. Nagle, hand in the air, mouth open in a shout. That sort of thing not only personalizes a story in a town like ours, but gives it focus.

What puzzled me, though, as I compared the two pieces, was the honesty of using the press in order to further one's own point of view. Do big-city newspapers, do television commentators and station owners use their power to forward the causes they approve of? And, if so, wasn't Robin terribly naïve in his instruction to *me?*

# 10.

Darryl von Vrock is a very confident young man. So secure, in fact, that he seems to assume that a girl would naturally be intrigued by him simply because he's there.

Worse, he's right. I mean, I am absolutely crazy for Martin—he's attractive and intelligent and dependable—but Darryl has something Martin hasn't. He's new.

And he's running this as far as it will take him.

I mean, I am not the first girl in our class he's laid siege to. And I'm certain I won't be the last.

Of course, I felt just the tiniest bit sleazy about indulging myself this way—in *letting* Darryl come on instead of saying firmly that I'm otherwise entangled. He knows that, of course. But it was really up to me to make the statement. I wondered why I found that so difficult.

The trick with Darryl, I decided, was to stay detached. Not to let him *know* you're viewing the moment objectively, but to stay secretly distant. You can watch his face, his hands, his body; you can listen to him pour it on, hearing the insincerity of it all just below the anguished truth—and you can choose to accept it or not.

He is amusing, I'll give him that. Not funny: amusing. He makes me smile. He also makes me feel terrifically smart and, because of the distance between us, superior. I don't think this is what he has in mind when he turns on his generator.

My folks were out this particular evening, away for dinner and a few hours with friends. Georgia had beaten me to the punch by asking permission to go out after supper, leaving me with the unenviable task of baby-sitting with Jonny. Not that he required a lot of attention, really. He went directly upstairs after I fed him and did his homework and probably, if habit holds true, spent the rest of the night making up chemical formulae to blow down the house, or up. Which he almost did last year with a Christmas chemistry set. He had been sitting on the floor in the den, mixing and matching elements and metals and powders and colored substances, and then lighting them. There was a tremendous explosion, and whatever had been in his vial went straight up to the ceiling, and then straight down, missing Jonny himself by inches but also splatting all over the rug and making it a thing of many colors.

Since I was temporarily beached for the evening and since I had promised I would see Darryl one night, there was nothing to do but invite him over when he suggested it. And the minute he walked in, I could trace his thoughts.

"You all alone?" he asked, walking around the room, testing, I suppose, its acoustics and its exits. He is long and tall and thin, but not gangly. His hair is red and ruler-straight. His eyes are brown, flecked with amber, and his skin is not the white you would expect with someone so fair; it's darker, older-looking, as though it were used to rough treatment. It may have been, since he had arrived in Owanka only a few months before from Kansas City, his father having been transferred from there to here to take over the new Younkers store out at the mall.

"My brother Jonny's upstairs," I told him, sitting down at one end of a couch and watching him circulate. He grinned. "He's the young one, right?" he asked.

I nodded. God, boys can be so transparent!

Darryl sat down on the same couch, although he did not instantly slide across at me. "I've really wanted to see you," he said intensely.

I laughed. "You do, every day."

"You know what I mean, Ava," Darryl said softly. "Alone. Somewhere we could...talk..."

I nodded. "Well, this is it. Your big chance."

He ducked his head and grinned and then raised just his eyes, looking up at me under his lashes. "You're a truly beautiful girl," he said whispering.

I smiled. "Thank you."

"I mean that," he insisted. "That's not just a line."

He reached out and took one of my hands in his. I did not object. Yet. "And your skin is so smooth," he said, still whispering.

"Wouldn't you like to ask a few questions first?" I wanted to know, teasing of course, but I really didn't see this as an opportunity to make out, what with who knew who coming in at any moment. Also, I admit, I do prefer a little warm-up.

He leaned away from me, still holding my hand. "No, I don't think so," he said after a moment. "I mean, I've seen you. I know what you do, how you sound, where you go." He paused. "I think we could make a sensational team, Ava."

I was so surprised I nearly laughed out loud. I might have in a second more, but the telephone rang. "Excuse me," I said, pulling my hand free and standing to walk into the hallway where a telephone sat on a small marble-topped table. "Hello?" I said.

"May I speak with Ava Van Buren, please?" It was a woman's voice, young-sounding but not one of my friends.

"This is she."

"Oh, hi. This is Susan Woods. From the *Herald?*"

"Oh yes, I know you," I said, and then I blushed. "I mean, I've read your work."

"And I've just finished reading yours," she said.

I wasn't sure how to respond so I just waited.

"You did a good job on that Council meeting," Susan Woods said then. "I was really impressed, Ava."

"Well, thank you very much."

"It set me thinking," she went on. "We could work together on this story, you know? I mean, there you are, right at the heart and soul of this whole argument. It's one thing for me to report from the outside, but to have someone inside the school like you, someone who can write, who notices things and is articulate, well, I think that would just be an unbeatable combination."

"You do?" Suddenly, I was part of everyone's ideal union.

"Yes, I truly do. Are you going to be home sometime over the weekend? I mean, I'd really like to come out and talk to you about this, sort of kick a few ideas around, see where they lead us."

"Why don't you come over now?" I suggested, almost breathless with excitement, and completely forgetting Darryl in the other room.

"Oh no," Susan said. "I'd hate to break into your evening that way."

"You wouldn't be, really," I lied, remembering. Let Darryl eat his heart out.

"You're sure?"

"I'm just sitting around with a friend from school. My folks are out and I'm saddled with my youngest brother."

"Well, if you really wouldn't mind, I'd love to get together to map a strategy."

Wow! She was already counting on me!

"Have you got our address?" I asked.

"From the phone book," she told me. "I'll be there in about ten minutes. And I *promise* I won't stay long."

"Don't promise," I said. "Just walk in and start talking." Then I laughed. "Really, I'm flattered."

"You should be," Susan Woods said, laughing in return.

"Well, I *am*," I told Darryl defensively.

"Well, *I'm* not," he moped. "How can you do that to us?"

"'Us'?" I was surprised and just a little annoyed. "Listen, all I've done is tell someone she's welcome to stop by to chat for a while. Surely that isn't going to give you hives or cramps or whatever unsatisfied boys claim they get."

"That's hitting low," Darryl said, but with a grin.

"You're not my first would-be seducer," I said, pleased now that he was taking it all in good humor. "I've gone a few rounds with the best of them."

"Not yet, you haven't," Darryl claimed, reaching out toward me and grabbing my shoulders, pulling me toward him.

*Oh, what the hell?* I thought, letting him kiss me. It was early in the game, but it served a purpose. Did I want to see this boy again? I thought a moment, and tasted. Yes.

"Who was that on the phone?" Jonny called from upstairs.

Darryl and I broke apart quickly.

"Just a friend," I called back. "Nothing special."

"No *one* special," Jonny corrected, and then we heard his feet clomping back toward his own bedroom.

"Smart kid," Darryl judged. "Not only is he right, but he's invisible. Very classy."

I laughed and the doorbell rang.

"You can stay if you want," I told him.

"Let's see how it goes," Darryl considered. "I mean, I'm not really involved in this battle."

I went to the front door and pulled it open. Susan Woods stood on the threshold, a lightweight cashmere sweater thrown over her shoulders, her thin lips parted in a broad, generous smile. "Hi, Ava," she said, sticking out her hand and taking mine to shake it. "I'm really glad to meet you."

"Come in," I said, pumping away and then standing back so she could walk into the house ahead of me. From behind, I noticed she was the slightest bit overweight. This was offset, though, by her style: direct, straightforward, her eyes never leaving your own as she spoke or listened. Also, she had an astonishingly clear, creamy complexion that anyone would envy.

She walked ahead of me and automatically took the proper turn to go into the den. Darryl was standing there, not at all ill at ease, a smile on his face. It hit me immediately: an "older" woman, another challenge. I introduced them and Susan sat where I'd been sitting on the couch. Darryl took a small chair nearby.

"Can I get you something?" I asked, ever the perfect hostess. "A drink, or some coffee?"

"Coffee would be nice," Susan said. "If it's no bother."

"It's no bother because it's instant. I'll just put on the water."

I left Darryl alone to make whatever headway he could, or that he wanted to, and went to the kitchen, filled the kettle with water, and set it on the burner. I walked slowly back into the den where apparently things were moving slowly, for Darryl sat where I'd left him, and Susan seemed perfectly poised on the couch.

Neither one looked as though he or she had fallen instantly in love. Not that I particularly cared.

"I promised I wouldn't stay long," Susan said as I sat beside her, keeping one ear open for the whistle from the kitchen. "So let's get right down to business, O.K.?"

"Fine with me," I said easily, though I was excited inside.

"I'd like us to work together on this *Grapes of Wrath* story," she said directly. "After all, I can attend town meetings, or do interviews, but you're right there on the scene, on the battlefield. Without you, without your dispatches," and she smiled at her own turn of phrase, "I'm just covering the home front. And that's simply not good enough."

"I really don't think I can help all that much," I said. "I mean, most kids aren't that concerned. At least, not so far."

"It's more than just the kids, just the people in your class or Georgia's," she replied. Then I thought: *Wait a minute! How did she know about Georgia?* "It's what happens among the teachers, too. I mean, they're more than just teachers. They're parents, too, many of them. They'll have their personal points of view, and it will be almost impossible, I'd think, for them to keep their private feelings from their professional ones in this case."

"I don't think they'll share much of what they feel with *me*," I said honestly.

"They may not have to," Susan Woods said with a sort of sly glimmer in her eyes. "You're perceptive. And you're literate. You're more than smart enough to read signs for yourself and to draw conclusions."

I was pleased she said that. "There's just one thing," I said slowly. "I mean, is drawing conclusions really fair? In writing for a newspaper, I mean? After all, theoretically I'm just supposed to report the news, straight and without frills. Wouldn't drawing conclusions, as you say, be sort of immoral?"

Susan frowned and then brightened. "I'm going to let you in on a trade secret," she said. "It's just as impossible for reporters to keep their personal biases out of their work as it is teachers, no matter how hard we try. I mean, even the selection of the news features we do more or less indicates our own interests. Unless, of course, we've been routinely assigned and sent out."

"You mean *your* mind is already made up?" I asked.

"Of course it is," she answered quickly. "It has to be. After all, what's at stake here isn't just one book, or one set of opinions. It's the freedom of choice. And freedom of the press, too. I'd be cutting off my own nose if I didn't understand that and do what I could to make other people see it, too."

"The power of the Fourth Estate," Darryl interjected suddenly, sounding very sage and laid back. "Newspapers do more than report, they *persuade*."

"Exactly," Susan agreed quickly. "And if the particular paper has acted responsibly, and written and lobbied quietly and honestly over the years, people have a tendency to trust it. It's not just a matter of persuading, actually," she decided then. "It's more an educational process. We bring the rest of the world into someone's home and tell him how it affects him. We have a touch more objectivity than the average reader, perhaps, because we try hard to look at the Big Picture. But what we're always trying to do, underneath everything else, is inform."

I nodded, confused a little. I guessed I *had* always believed what I read in the newspapers.

"Now, getting down to cases," Susan continued, "surely you know where you stand in all this?"

"Surely," I echoed, feeling suddenly fainthearted and weak.

"Well?" she waited pleasantly.

I nodded, stalling. "Yes...I know where I stand...I mean, I agree with you."

"And with Georgia?" she added, unnecessarily, I thought.

"I suppose," I agreed. "Although I'm not the firebrand she is."

"Which, for our purposes, is just as well. After all, we want you to be discreet, to be subtle."

I grinned. "Am I going undercover?"

Susan Woods laughed. "In a way," she allowed. "Not that you ever have to deny what you're doing, why you're asking questions, if anyone pesters you. But yes, in a way. By keeping your ears open and your eyes, you can sense and then tell me how other kids are reacting to all this, what they think their parents are feeling, on whose side their families are likely to vote. I think, as time passes, a lot of information like that will surface. People have a tendency to repeat and take their parents' points of view for their own."

"What exactly am I supposed to be doing?" I asked. "Do you want me to write articles for you?"

"I'm not sure, yet," Susan admitted. "First of all, I want the sources. I want you to keep notes of people you've heard or spoken with, in addition to what they're saying or thinking. Teachers, kids, Miss McCandless, anyone who opens up and volunteers. If you can *get* people to do that, that's even better. You'll be covering the story anyway for *The Hawk,* so it's not as though you'd be sneaking around spying on people. You would just be giving me more resource, more information, so that the stories the *Herald* prints are fuller and better rounded than they might be."

"Will Ava get her own by-line?" Darryl asked suddenly, an odd smile playing on his lips. "Will she be credited at all?"

Susan looked quickly up at him and then away just as quickly. "Naturally," she said firmly. "It may take a little time, of course. But there's no reason why she couldn't be acknowledged."

"'Well-placed sources, wishing to remain anonymous'?" Darryl prodded.

"Are you suggesting that Ava not help me in this?" Susan Woods asked severely.

"That's a dodge," Darryl said. "I just think since you're laying everything out so clearly, you ought to lay out the whole thing."

"Look," I interjected quickly, aware of a tension in the room I didn't understand and which I also didn't like, "if what you're doing is worthwhile and you believe in it, why then, you believe in it, period. Who cares about credits?"

"Right!" Susan agreed happily. "That's the way we *all* feel."

In an odd way, that was a warming sentiment: to be included in that "we all" meant that I was part of the hard-working, devoted press corps. I could live with that.

"I'll be happy to help," I said then.

Susan stood up and clapped her hands together. "Perfect!" she said eagerly. "That's what I'd hoped you'd say. Now then, there's not much we want to worry about just yet. It'll take a day or two for the steam to start to build. But we'll keep in touch. I'll keep my ears to the railroad tracks downtown, and you keep yours on the hallways. I know, why don't we have lunch on Saturday?"

"I work on Saturdays," I said. "At Chez Elle."

"Perfect, that's just across the street from the *Herald*. We can have a bite together and see where we are by week's end."

"All right," I said, standing then, too.

"You're wonderful to help, Ava," Susan said as she started from the den to the hallway. "Oh, and also, in case I forgot to tell you this, I *did* like your article. I thought it was very professional. I *know* we're going to be the Woodward and Bernstein of Owanka."

"The Redford and Hoffman," I echoed enthusiastically.

"So, what do you think?" I asked Darryl after Susan had left the house.

"I thought she was pretty clever," he said.

"What do you mean?"

"Buttering you up like that, making you feel important and talented."

"Well, maybe I am," I said angrily.

"Maybe you are," he allowed. "But mostly what you are is gullible, and therefore useful."

"You're being purposely hurtful," I complained.

"No, you're being dense," Darryl judged. "She's using you. Now, that's fine with me if you know it and agree to it in advance. That's all I was trying to say," he added, softening a bit, coming across the room to put his hands on my shoulders. "I think what you're doing is fine as long as you keep your eyes open on your own behalf, as well as *The Hawk*'s."

"What is this?" I asked, still angry. "The Kansas City oracle?"

Darryl grinned and shook his head. "You know, Ava, girls mature faster than boys. I mean, the whole world knows that. What people forget is that a boy's world is different, a little rougher, a little more real. That's all I'm saying. You may be more mature; I'm less starry-eyed. That's all."

"Huh!" I was not appeased.

"Come on," Darryl urged, teasing a little, "you've got two days before you go off to the front lines. Give me a little kiss."

I couldn't help myself. Despite the fact that I was really very angry at what Darryl had said about being taken in, he *was* sort of appealing just then. And new. So I gave him a kiss.

What I decided, standing in the doorway watching Darryl walk to his car, was that I wasn't sure I actually *liked* him very much. Putting aside his physical pull, he did seem rough and suspicious and, also, too sure of himself. And of me.

And then I suddenly remembered the coffee we never had. I closed the front door and rushed back into the kitchen. Perfect! I'd done everything but turn on the gas under the kettle. Oh, well.

Standing there in the kitchen, I realized that more important than whether or not I actually liked Darryl just then, if *he* liked me, he should have supported me— if he cared at all—instead of knocking me down.

Martin would have.

# 11.

It's amazing how, despite the fact you think you understand what's going on, so often you can be wrong.

To me it seemed the next few days were peaceful. Certainly I never imagined the turmoil beneath the calm. As far as I could tell, the battlefield was quiet, so quiet one would never have known there were people getting ready for a war at all.

Which just goes to show how perceptive I am. Of course things seemed serene to me because I wanted them to be that way. I hadn't forgotten to keep my ears and eyes open at school prior to the Saturday date I had with Susan Woods. But the halls there seemed no more noisy or frantic than before; I saw no little groups whispering and planning, gesturing, looking over their shoulders; I got wind of no organized opposition or defense. Sharks practices continued; classes went on; the football team worked out every afternoon and a pep rally was held that Friday night.

It wasn't until that Saturday morning, as I grabbed a quick breakfast before heading down to Chez Elle, that I realized how blind I'd been. True enough, I had known Georgia belonged to Miss McCandless' Reading Club at school, and that she, like the rest of us at her age, was active in the Luther League. But I hadn't begun to suspect how busy she'd been planting seeds, watering them, talking sweetly and hopefully to them, second by second urging them to germinate, until I opened the *Herald* that morning.

> Gentlemen:
>
> As you have reported, there is a drive in our community to censor the freedom to read of Owanka's younger citizens.
>
> Without making personal accusations of motive on the part of those members of the City Council who approve and support this measure, I wanted others to know that a choice does still exist, and can, if we all work together.
>
> To that aim, I am soliciting support— moral as well as financial—for FIRIF (Freedom Is Reading Is Freedom). Inquiries and/or donations may be sent to me at the address below, or to Mr. Donald Arrand, c/o Owanka National Growers Bank.
>
> Georgia Van Buren

To say I was mortified, embarrassed, and furious is understatement. What we don't need in our family is an activist, certainly not someone who is going to make stands and take positions so publicly. I mean, one can imagine writing such a letter, but sending it? Of course, Georgia had help. How much I didn't yet understand.

To complicate matters further, the *Herald* printed a second letter.

Gentlemen:

There is a divisive, corrosive, and inflammatory movement organizing in Owanka of which you are clearly aware. I refer to the position taken by Mr. Fairchild Brady of the City Council, et al., that he (and they) know what books are best for our children to read.

I have seen entire communities disrupted and destroyed by attempts at censorship such as this, extending even to trying to legislate or force whole families to conform to so-called community standards.

I urge every man and woman who believes in freedom and fair play and the right of personal choice on which this country is founded to fight Mr. Brady's proposition, and to vote, on November 4th, to defeat his attempt to fiat fundamental freedoms in our city.

Urgently,

> Rev. Robert E. Fickett
> Owanka Methodist Church

When I met Susan Woods at Morrie's for lunch that day, she was wearing an enormous smile. I couldn't help but smile in return, though not with a lot of genuine glee.

"It's happening, Ava," she said to me as we slid into a booth. "I knew it would take a few days, but boy-oh-boy! Are we going to have a battle royal on our hands!"

"What makes you so pleased?" I asked. "I can see it's

a good story, but really, Susan, I'm not sure it's anything to be joyous about."

"No, of course not," she agreed, hedging just a little as she picked up a menu and quickly scanned it. "I don't mean to sound as though I'm gloating. It's just that this is the kind of story that can really explode, really give you a chance to show your stuff."

"Did you see the two letters in the paper this morning?" I asked.

She nodded eagerly. "You wouldn't believe how many others there are we *didn't* print," she admitted happily. "Oh, Ava, this is going to be a carnival!"

"What happens if Mr. Brady wins?" I wondered.

"But don't you see?" Susan asked, leaning across the table to explain. "It doesn't make any difference. One way or the other we have a battle here that can echo all across the state, all across the country! I mean, you don't imagine Owanka is the only town in America to feel this way, do you?"

I shrugged. "I haven't thought about it," I admitted.

"Well, do, for just a moment," Susan suggested. "Listen, the whole general election's being fought along these very same lines. 'America's fallen on its ass... we have to return to the old values... God loves the devout but He respects the doer... America *has* to be what it once was, leader of the free world, caller of the shots, the most righteous, the strongest...' I mean, that's what's happening now, Ava. That's the choice the pols give us. Make no mistake. What's going on here, Mr. Brady's crusade to clean up the schools, that's only a symptom of other conflicts across the country."

"You mean we're part of the Big Picture?" I asked, smiling a little sadly.

"Sure, wait and see," Susan said easily.

"You think Mr. Brady will win?"

She nodded. "Not enough to make bets on it yet, but probably."

"I wonder if Georgia sees all this the same way you do."

"Probably not in the same terms," Susan allowed. "But you can bet your bottom dollar the Reverend Mr. Fickett does."

I grimaced a little. "I'm not sure his letter is going to do what he wants. I mean, well and good, go out and fight. But to bring a church into it, even just by writing its name at the bottom of a letter, well, that seems a little risky to me."

"Wait, wait," Susan cautioned happily. "That's just the beginning. If one church takes a stand, others will have to. And businesses and unions and families and you name it. In four weeks the whole town will be two armed camps."

"Did you know the Bradys are Methodists?"

"Ohmygod!" Susan laughed, clapping her hands. "What a face-off!"

I frowned. "You make this sound like *fun*," I said.

"But it is!" Susan said quickly. "Maybe it's just the difference in our points of view," she allowed, shoving the menu across the table at me. "For me, I guess, it's exciting because it's so far-reaching, so *indicative*. Also, of course, it's a story you can really sink your teeth into."

For just the slightest fraction of a second I had a sudden sympathy for the unlamented Richard M. Nixon.

# 12.

One almost immediate effect of the Council's newly passed proposition was an increase in the number of candidates for the City Council itself. It was as though, without meaning to, Mr. Brady had opened a door to a small private party and was being swamped by a lot of starving peasants whose manners were rough but whose eyes were fixed on the banquet table.

The way Council elections are run is simple. Anyone may announce his or her availability for office and make a run, because seats are ultimately awarded those whose vote is largest. Which is to say, the five biggest vote-getters on any slate are winners. We don't have people running head-to-head against each other. We have people running on their own, putting forward their own ideas for reform or change and hoping that sufficient numbers of their fellow citizens will agree with what they have in mind.

In this particular November's election, the candidates had already announced by the time Mr. Brady edged his proposal through the Council. Which meant that the newcomers were write-in candidates capitalizing on the electorate's last minute realization that something important was in the air. With an issue suddenly uncovered, with emotions unleashed, the choices dramatically increased from an ordinary ten candidates (including the incumbents) to nearly twenty within three days. "Politicians" emerged from the woodwork, materializing before our very eyes, asking for support, more frequently decrying the ideas of a certain section of the existing Council. The division was simple. Either one was for or against Mr. Brady's proposition. If a voter indicated he or she disapproved of legislated reading, he or she was soon besieged by phone calls, home visits, invitations to small gatherings to hear and meet a candidate who, generally, had been for all the years previous someone you knew as a family druggist, a garage mechanic, a Sunday school teacher.

Suddenly, Owanka found out that it cared deeply—not only about reading and what was suitable for its children to read, but also about what many felt was the country's drift toward immorality, an inequity in taxes, the posture of America in relation to its allies abroad, the intrusion of government into everyone's daily lives (which, in its own way, was mirrored exactly in Mr. Brady's proposal to begin with).

What people did not usually speak of publicly—religion, politics, money—surfaced in everyday conversations, and therefore those conversations became heated and angry and divisive.

On the following Monday after Georgia's letter soliciting funds appeared in the *Herald,* Mr. Donald Arrand came out of his house to get into his car to drive to the bank, and found that all four tires on it had been slashed during the night. Mr. Arrand is a generally quiet, well-spoken man in his mid-forties. He did not turn purple or begin to shout. He went back into his house to call the city's three-car taxi company and took a cab to the bank. For the next five weeks, his Mercedes stayed in his driveway, where it looked as though it were hunkering down on its haunches, deep in thought. I guess he decided that it would serve as a reminder, almost a memorial, that way. (Also, of course, why have the tires replaced when the same thing could happen over again?)

The members of the Council themselves met their new challengers as differently as their personalities would have led one to imagine. For example, Amos Allen made no speeches, went to no rallies, canvassed at no bazaars. His attitude was clearly stated in one article in the *Herald:* "People know me, and they know how I think. If they don't like it, then it's up to them to change it."

Mrs. Irene Clarke, always looking fresh and cool, flirting a little with her audiences, was dismayed that Owanka's once quiet, leafy streets should be littered by flyers and handouts, with harangues from loud-speaker trucks—these last imported from Iowa City or Des Moines. She never for one minute wanted to say anything against Mr. John Steinbeck. She simply thought he had been ill-advised to let his imagination flow quite so freely.

The two most prominent voices in the campaign belonged to Stanley Sopwith, clearly a founding father of the local New Right, and to Mrs. George Nichols, who felt strongly that the issue was an affront to her School Board Committee's prerogatives and duties.

Stanley Sopwith was invited to appear before the Rotary Club, and the Kiwanis, and the Chamber of Commerce. He gave the same speech over and over, varying its emphases sometimes, but always ending with a call to valor, patriotism, to America first, last, best, and always.

Mrs. Nichols would follow, speaking to the same groups, explaining heatedly that Stanley's view of life

was barbaric, unreasonable, prejudicial, racist, chau-
vinist.

But it wasn't just Stanley Sopwith Mrs. Nichols was
after. She took on the Moral Majority, the New Right,
the failure of Washington to provide leadership. What
in fact was happening day by day was that Mrs. Nichols
talked about Owanka, but addressed the world. She
was entering Politics, though most of us didn't see this
immediately. Actually, for a while it just seemed she
had flipped out.

Above all this, standing at the top of Olympus gazing
down at us mortals was Fairchild Brady, totally convinced that what he was doing was right. Make that
Right; the capital makes a difference. Because a lot of
people agreed with him. If one kept one's eyes on the
real issue, on the single factor that caused all this confusion and revived civic ardor, what Mr. Brady offered
his followers was their first chance in years to change
their own lives. I could see this in my own father. Others
saw it as clearly, and while many of them may not have
been overfond of Fairchild Brady, nonetheless they
were seriously considering taking this first opportunity
to Make a Difference, to Turn the Country Around, to
start to Slow Creeping Immorality and Public Dishon-
esty.

Not that Daddy ever said his mind was made up.

But we had all been put on warning by his silence.
No announcement was ever issued to us, but the strain
around the house continued and increased until it
seemed a curtain had been put between him and the
rest of us. He smiled and joked and behaved normally,
and he did no campaigning of his own. But he did not
want to discuss It with us.

One evening Georgia lured me into attending one
of her fund-raising meetings. She was off to attend a
gathering that was chaired by Mr. Arrand, and where

a number of people our family had known for years
would be. The purpose of the evening was to try to
examine dispassionately, if possible, the list of twenty
candidates and to identify clearly, once and for all,
those for Brady's proposition, and hence censorship,
and those against it. As Mr. Arrand said that night,
coming out as a group for candidates was admittedly
risky, since any member of the Council eventually
would become more than just a single-issue public ser-
vant. But choices had to be made, chances taken.

Susan Woods was also at the meeting, and afterward
she told me how much she admired the Opposition, as
she insisted on calling Mr. Arrand's group, for taking
and accepting the help of absolutely anyone who was
able-bodied and willing. By which she meant Georgia
and her coterie of pals solicited initially from Miss
McCandless' Reading Club and our own Luther League.

For it was true that when someone Georgia's age
had something to say, he or she was recognized as an
adult and listened to with attention and very little
sense of isn't he/she cute? Furthermore, Georgia and
her crew were allowed to vote on the final selection of
candidates FIRIF would support. I was impressed, not
just with Mr. Arrand's ability to run a meeting, but
also with some of Georgia's friends to whom I hadn't
paid that much attention before.

In any case, when the meeting was over, Georgia
and I walked home. The night was a warm one. We
were having a spell of Indian summer and the early
October night was sweet with the scent of leaves and
cut grass and late-blooming climbing roses.

"You know, Ava, you can't go on playing the objective observer much longer," Georgia told me as we
strolled.

"Why not? That's what I am."

"Even newspeople," Georgia said, tapping my arm,

"sooner or later find themselves alone in a voting booth. I mean, you think Walter Cronkite doesn't vote?"

"I'm sure Walter and I would see eye to eye," I guessed. "Listen, Georgia, it's not that I'm unimpressed with what *you're* doing, and how *you* feel. But for myself, well, just as you have to allow other people to make up their minds and vote however they will, you have to give me the same freedom."

"But doesn't your blood boil, just a little? I mean, you understand what's at stake here. Doesn't Mr. Brady make you the tiniest bit mad?"

"As far as I can see, getting *angry* is the last thing anyone needs. The whole town's already frothing at the mouth. Besides, you've got more than enough people to work with without having me by your side."

"But that's where you should be!" Georgia shouted. "Look, we have the same parents, the same standards, the same habits. How could we *not* agree and work together for something as important as this?"

"I'm not sure that what happens here in Owanka—" I started to say, but Georgia cut me off, still shouting.

"You drive me up a wall!" she shrieked. "I'm asking for a commitment, I'm asking you to work for something very, very important. How can you be like this? What good does it do to stay so damned distant!"

"I don't notice Rick running home to dig in," I said.

"No." Georgia quieted, crestfallen. "Robin understands, though. Maybe Rick hasn't got so much time."

"He's living a different life now, Georgia," I said. "He's away from home. This doesn't matter to him any more. Robin comes back and goes to your meetings and takes things back to Iowa City to Xerox for you on the sly because...well, mostly, I think, because of you, of how he feels about you and what you're doing. But Rick's always been more independent, more likely to go his own way. If *I* fall somewhere in between the two, I don't think you can legitimately complain. Now, do you, honestly?"

Georgia looked at me a moment and then threw her head back, mouth agape, and uttered the most frustrated, constipated sound I've ever heard. I don't even know how one would spell it.

She sighed—noisily—and we turned a corner, starting for our house, which was only about a hundred yards away.

"Ah, the home fires still burn," Georgia said.

"Late news, probably," I said.

We ambled up the front walk and onto the front porch. And then we both stopped and stood absolutely still, as though squinting into the shadows. Not so much to see, which would have been impossible without X-ray vision, but to make clearer the sounds we heard.

What reached us was *tone,* tone and rhythm, and volume. Not that anyone inside was shouting. I don't think my parents have ever shouted, at us, at each other. But the tenor of their voices rose and fell in a staccato tempo, my father's slower and deeper in color, my mother's rising and faster. I reached out and grabbed hold of Georgia's arm to make sure she made no sound, did not move.

"But she's right!" my mother was saying. "I mean, my God, Fred, of course you can see that!"

"... be right for herself ... not making judgments like that."

"That is just cowardice!"

"Alva, listen to yourself. You don't mean that."

"... probably not ... but what about what we believe in ... years and years?"

"Are you talking about choice?" my father asked.

Georgia was rigid.

"Well, of course I am!" my mother argued, her voice rising once more.

"Well then, remember please that choice extends in both directions. I have as much right to my choice as Georgia does to hers."

"Fred, can you honestly sit there and tell me with a straight face that you believe censorship is a good thing?"

"I am not discussing censorship," my father started to say.

"You most certainly are!" Mother said quickly. "There just isn't any other word. What you're advocating is censorship, pure and simple."

"What I'm advocating is the reasonable expectation of any parent to protect his children from what he thinks harmful."

"Georgia is fourteen, for heaven's sakes," Mother said. "By the time she gets to tenth grade, she'll be fifteen. You're not telling me now, years after both Rick and Robin had the same experience, that you think they were damaged irreparably by reading this book?"

"No, I'm not," Father replied evenly.

"If you tell me it's because they're boys, Fred, I am going to throw something at you."

Father laughed.

"Well, what's the difference, then?" Mother insisted.

"Listen, darling, the way I feel has nothing at all to do with either the book or the particular child," Father said slowly. "All I'm saying is that times have changed, and I'm not sure I like *how* they've changed. I want the children to see the old values cherished once more. I want our kids to grow and to learn and to become good citizens. I don't want them to see immorality and cheating and crime as everyday occurrences that have to be lived with."

"Come on!" Mother was exasperated. "What you're

talking about can hardly be achieved by refusing to let
children read books."

"You don't know that," Father reasoned. "None of
us does. Who knows what influences a child? What
causes him to see the world in a particular light? Sure,
we try to be good parents, but we're not the only people
with whom he comes into contact. We're not the only
models for life, for work and marriage. He sees everyone else's parents. As he grows, he sees his friends. He
makes up his own mind."

"Precisely!" Mother said happily. "That's exactly
what I've been trying to say. This whole thing is just
burying your head in the sand. You can't seriously believe, Fred, that *The Grapes of Wrath* is going to color
Georgia's perception of becoming an adult."

"Of course it will," Father defended. "Of course it
will, just as any other book she reads will."

"So what are you going to do? Make her stop reading?"

"No," Father said somberly. "I'm just going to try to
make certain that what she reads presents a picture
of the world that I can live with."

"*You?*" Mother nearly shouted. "*Your* picture of the
world? What do you want, carbon copies? Who are you
protecting? Georgia, or yourself?"

"We're not such bad originals, Alva," Father replied,
ducking the second question.

Mother laughed, not unkindly, but laugh she did.
"Are you standing there, telling me that your parents
forced their view of the world onto their son? I mean,
think, Fred, *think!* You were the first Van Buren ever
to go to college. Surely your parents had confidence in
you, had some feeling that you were able to fend for
yourself, make your own decisions, live with them?
Make your own mistakes, as the saying goes, and survive?"

My father was silent.

"They trusted you to make your own friends, didn't they?" Mother went on. "They let you choose me, for heaven's sakes. I mean, who knew then? Perhaps I would have corrupted you."

"And so you did," said Father very quietly, just loudly enough to be heard out-of-doors.

By this time, Georgia was shaking where she stood. I felt the tremors in her arm and gripped her more firmly than before.

"There's just one more string to my bow," said Mother then.

"What's that?" asked Father.

"I can't stop you from voting for the proposal. I can't, and wouldn't stop you from talking with the kids about this. But I think you ought to know that the way you feel is directly opposed to everything I've ever felt or thought or wanted from life. I don't believe in censorship. I don't believe books can be harmful to a child. A child brings his own experiences to what he reads. If it's pornography he's got in front of him, unless he understands what's going on, sooner or later he's going to put the thing aside and get on with his life. I believe, Fred, and I mean this, I believe that words are precious and stories more valuable than gold. And if you carry this outside this house, if you get up in church and take a public stand, then I want you on notice that I will do the same, more loudly, more angrily, and I'll campaign day and night. You'll learn to cook or starve. You'll learn to operate the washing machine, and to vacuum and to dust and to shop for food. And once I get going, who knows? Maybe I'll just sign on with Louise Nichols and work my way to the statehouse."

My father laughed then. "That's censorship," he complained.

"You're damned right!" Mother answered. "This can cut both ways."

"Ohhh, Alva," said my father.

"Don't ohhh, Alva me," said my mother.

"Ohhhh!" Georgia under her breath, breaking my grip and reaching for the screendoor. "I am going to go in there and—"

I reached out quick as a snake and spun her around. "If you even open that door one inch," I whispered at her, "I am going to make a real case for censorship and punch out your tiny brain!"

# 13.

Charles Kuralt one day slipped into town to interview Fairchild Brady. Also, to be fair, he talked with Benjamin Nagle and Miss McCandless, and during the narration of his report there was a five-second film clip of Georgia and her chums in the Reading Club.

The points of view offered were predictable but we watched the CBS evening news with apprehension and excitement.

Mr. Brady held forth as a saintly village elder, concerned lest youth be compromised by what he termed unnecessary realism in literature. Mr. Nagle upheld the opposing view, although rather more loudly and a little less elegantly. And Miss McCandless tried her very best to put the whole matter in perspective by saying that if there were anything on the Depression that even faintly resembled the artistry of Mr. Steinbeck's novel, she for one would gladly stock it. But there wasn't and the Depression was neither hateful nor harming nor diseased; it was part of our national past and therefore an apt area for study.

One thing struck me as I listened to Charles Kuralt's folksy, dangerously slow approach to his subjects. No one, at least until that time, had thought to ask Mr. Claffin, the tenth-grade teacher whose reading list had brought all this upon our heads, what *he* thought, whether *he* still stood firm, whether *he* was caving in.

So I did. I made an appointment to interview him for *The Hawk*—Susan Woods be damned! It was my idea and a good one, I was convinced.

Mr. Claffin is a man of about thirty, newly married and with a small baby boy. He had come to Owanka from the school system in Clinton, not too far upriver. He seemed shy and boyish to me, almost surprised that someone should come to him and ask what he thought, having lit the fuse.

"Well," I said soon after I sat down across from him in his classroom, "you *did* light it."

He blushed and shook his head. "Not really. The book was on the syllabus already. It seemed to me a good one to read. I simply kept it on and assigned it."

"When was the last time you read the book, all the way through?" I asked.

"I read everything before we study it," he said. "If I started to rely on notes or lectures or ideas I'd used before, I'd bore myself and I'd bore my classes. Besides, when you reread something like this, new ideas always surface."

"Were you ever disturbed by the language in the book?"

He shook his head again. "Not really. I mean, Steinbeck doesn't start out swearing on page one. He leads you into the lives of his characters and then lets you listen to them speak. Besides, there are whole chunks of the book—mostly about Ma Joad—where there's no profanity at all."

"Would you assign the book again if you could?"

He smiled. "Ah well," he hedged. "You mean, if I knew what was going to happen, would I?"

I nodded.

"I'd like to think I would, Ava," he said quietly. "But

'm honestly not sure. I mean, a lot of strange things have happened since all this began."

"How do you mean, strange?"

"Well," and he blushed, hesitating to confide in me, I guess. "The usual sorts of intimidations, you know."

"No, I don't know," I admitted flatly. "What do you mean?"

He grinned a little sheepishly. "Late-night telephone calls, anonymous letters, that sort of thing."

"Really?" I was astonished. "But why? Who?"

"Who I can't tell you," Mr. Claffin said almost sorrowfully. "The why is anybody's guess. I mean, after all, whatever damage is real has already been done. I'm out of it now, effectively. I mean, it's unlikely I'll assign anything I think is controversial in the future. At least for a while, anyway."

I wanted to jump up and shout, *There! You see? The damage?* But I didn't. Mr. Claffin ducked his head and continued. "I guess people just like to feel powerful and threatening and strong, and if it gives them pleasure, why, I guess I can stand it."

"But what about your wife, your baby?"

"My wife's a little nervous just now, but that will pass, I'm sure, before long."

"But this is awful!" I offered. "I mean, I can see threatening Mr. Brady or someone, but not a teacher!"

Mr. Claffin smiled genuinely. I didn't think it was patronizing; what it was was almost sweet, as though he were remembering his own youth. He said nothing.

I went back home thinking about our interview, ready to write it up, remembering that not all of Owanka revolved around *The Grapes of Wrath*. While Mr. Claffin's wife answered (or at least read) anonymous letters, my father went to his store, often working late (inflation strikes again!) and, in his own way, removing himself from tension at home.

Not that he and my mother had stopped speaking or argued behind closed doors. But Georgia began bringing her fight home with her nearly every afternoon in the guise of one new friend and fire-brand after the other. The Reading Club meetings were shifted from Owanka High's library to our den, and my mother dutifully prepared hot chocolate and soda and cookies for the group whenever Georgia led them in the front door. (Jonny's attitude toward this late afternoon invasion was unvarying: he grabbed something from the refrigerator and spun on his heels to spend time outside until dinner and a return to normalcy.)

We continued going to school, and to struggle over world history quizzes and French and math. Martin and his weight-lifting cronies practiced football every afternoon on the practice field behind school, and played games on Friday nights or on Saturdays, depending on the schedule and the weather. Owanka was having a good season. By the middle of October, we had won three games and lost only one.

We all listened to "Double Fantasy" and "Guilty," and "Love on The Rocks." We went on Saturday nights to different houses after the games to dance and sometimes have a beer and generally hang out. We worried about when the Iranian hostages would be released and felt continually cheated each time negotiations broke down.

But politics was in the air, and people who ordinarily had not a care in the world became suspicious and worried and found ogres under beds they had long since forgotten. To whit: Mrs. Beaman, my boss at Chez Elle, could hardly wait for a customer to leave before she broke into her new, rather shrill Concerned Citizen's Song.

"Now, I don't mean you should be paranoid, Ava," she would say to me on Saturdays, "but it's only common sense for an attractive girl like yourself to be armed in *some* way."

I stood silently, nodding.

"Really, women like us have to be constantly alert." She ducked behind a counter and lifted her purse, reaching into it and bringing out a can of Mace. "You never know when you might need this," she told me, waving it in the air in front of her breasts.

I smiled, trying hard not to laugh. The man who "desired" Mrs. Beaman was already blinded, despite her taste in clothes.

Not that Mrs. Beaman was any more radical than millions of other women, I suppose, but suddenly she was hot to organize an anti-rape clinic and raise money for the Patrolmen's Benevolent Society.

"We have simply got to tell the criminals that we won't take it any more," she would go on. "What this country needs is to get tough, to force people to learn to fear us again. You think Mr. Nixon would have put us in this position?"

I didn't want to point out that Mr. Nixon had been a great supporter of the Shah. Besides, whether Mrs. Beaman voted Republican or Democrat wasn't the point of my mentioning her at all. What I am trying, in my halting fashion, to show is that here is a woman, wealthy by reasonable standards, with a good life and all her needs seen to, never the victim of crime or swindle, and she—like millions of Americans—in the autumn of 1980 was on fire for change, a return to what she thought she remembered as the good old days, regardless of the idea that the world had changed and a return to those forgotten golden years was, plainly, impossible.

Still, there was not a lot of time just then for philosophizing or introspection. Despite outward appearances of life proceeding normally, too much was happening. The *Des Moines Register and Tribune* sent down a reporter who camped at the Holiday Inn for the last three weeks of the campaign, and who sent back dispatches to the state capital that tried to capture the entire range of public opinion in Owanka. Naturally, Susan Woods was thrilled to have a colleague on hand, and I was dragged along one evening to meet Michael Prue, who was a man not much older than Susan herself, whose father and mother had both worked on newspapers all their lives. Whereas Susan saw the battle of Owanka as a chance to report on a trend, something that was not singular, Michael Prue had an even more professional view of the world. He had in his briefcase clippings from the *New York Times,* from the *Chicago Tribune,* from the *Los Angeles Times* and the *Dallas Times Herald,* all of which mirrored similar debates and struggles around the countryside. Reading them, one was not hopeful of the outcome of our own civil war.

So while I hadn't forgotten about my interview with Mr. Claffin, when it finally appeared the next week in *The Hawk,* I was a little surprised by at least one reader's reaction.

"How could you do that to me?" Susan Woods demanded. "I mean, that's dynamite! How could you keep it from me?"

I smiled into the telephone, just a little. "Well, how did I know what he would say?"

"You had plenty of time afterward," she argued.

"I only promised to *help,*" I said with as much firmness as I could muster. "I didn't promise to turn over everything." Then I grinned to myself again. "I suppose you want to subpoena me and my notes?"

"Very funny," Susan said. "I'm not sure what this does to our working relationship."

"Why should it do anything?" I asked innocently.

"After all, *you* could have interviewed Mr. Claffin, too, if you'd thought of it."

There was a moment's silence on the line. "Well, promise me you won't go off on your own again this way," Susan said, rather weakly, I thought.

"I can't," I said honestly. "But next time I'll give you fair warning, O.K.?"

Another pause. "I guess it will have to be."

She did not say goodbye.

# 14.

Our "working relationship," as Susan put it, had not been all sunshine and blue skies.

I did my best, listening around school, eavesdropping on adults whenever I overheard a word about the special election issue. I tried always to supply correctly spelled surnames and give the proper addresses for the people I quoted. And for those I couldn't quote, people who asked me not to or, more usually, whose words I had, in effect, "bugged," I thought I was incredibly discreet and daring at disguising them. "An informed source," "an unnamed official," "wishing to remain anonymous." The newspapers I read were full of credits like these and I picked up the jargon and used it easily, feeling professional and cagey.

Susan Woods, however, didn't seem to think quite so highly of my sleuthing. Despite the fact that our cooperating was her idea, as time wore on there was less and less of what had been promised and more direct, rather stern commands. What happened was fairly simple, I suppose, and probably exactly what Darryl von Vrock had expected. Whenever Susan had too much to do, or her schedule was jammed, *I* was sent out to cover a meeting or a television appearance. That does *not* mean

I got to go to a studio (of which there weren't any in Owanka to begin with); what it meant was that I had to stay home and watch a particular newscast or interview program, take notes, and then rustle them across town to Susan who would then write them up in her own style, and under her own name, for the *Herald.* I never had enough courage, or, put another way, I never got angry enough to confront her with this. Darryl would have, I'm sure. But hiding behind her reports was, for the moment, good enough for me.

Because, to be honest, my reporting was beginning to have other effects.

For example, one Monday morning when I came into my homeroom class a little early, Sandra Balin—a friend, not my best, not my worst, just a friend, someone who, I *thought,* had always been content to follow rather than lead—came over to me all smiles and whispery questions.

"What's he like?" she asked, smiling broadly.

"Who?"

"Darryl."

I was a little surprised. I guess it showed on my face.

"People saw you at the movies last Friday," Sandra explained. "You can't expect to fool around and not get caught in a town this size."

"I was not fooling around!" I said angrily.

"You were at the movies, though," Sandra persisted. I nodded.

"Well," she pushed. "Come on. What's he like? Does he have a good line? Is he, you know, smooth? I mean, well, *you* know. Is he experienced?"

"You never asked me any of this about Martin," I said to her rather distantly.

Her dark eyebrows came together almost in a scowl. "Why would I?" she asked in turn. "I mean, you and Martin have been going together for years. People just grow together, you know. I mean, you're almost an old married couple. Who cares about that? It's Darryl who's new, after all."

I smiled. "New and not as much of a Romeo as I thought, if he hasn't got round to you yet."

I'm not very often mean that way, but honestly, what business of hers was it anyway? It was true, Darryl and I had gone to see *Halloween,* a scary, cheap horror show, just for the fun of it, and it was also true that there were moments in it when, despite how hard you tried to control yourself and your reactions, you just couldn't. What would be more natural than grabbing onto the arm of the person nearest you?

I admit there was more to my reply than just annoyance. I was just the slightest bit guilty about seeing Darryl at all, even on Fridays when Martin had to stay in training for a Saturday game. Martin and I had never discussed an "open" relationship. We'd never had to. We really did seem, to many, including ourselves I suppose, almost married, we'd been hanging around together so long. I don't think I viewed Darryl's coming on as anything other than fun and games.

Not that Martin wouldn't have known . As Sandra said, Owanka is a small place and sooner or later everyone knows everyone else, or at least has heard of him, so Martin probably knew I'd been out with Darryl. Still, he never once said a thing, which, if truth be told, made me feel all the smaller. Not that I would lie or deny anything. Still, I guess the whole thing sat on my chest like a stone.

Anyway, what I was trying to show was that after that confrontation with Sandra, her manner changed distinctly. Not because I'd been sharp, I found out one afternoon after Sharks practice. For the past few days Sandra had been purposely and visibly snubbing me, in the halls, at practice, in classes. Not that I minded particularly. She was attractive and fairly bright, but

her temper was fairly unsteady and people knew she
would swing with a wind whenever it suited her. I
mean, one wouldn't want to bet one's life on Sandra's
coming to the rescue when you really needed it.

So, after we were dressed and about to leave the
locker room, I was standing next to her locker and put
my hand on it to steady it as she brushed out her dark
hair.

"What's going on with you?" I asked nicely. I was
deliberately trying to sound unconcerned but thoughtful, curious but not rabid to know.

"Whatever do you mean?" she asked, her voice rising
in an imitation of something she had probably heard
or seen on television that she thought was terrifically
sophisticated.

"Nothing, except you seem to be pretty cool lately,"
I said. Then, realizing that that was too imprecise and
also, in a way, complimentary, I added, "Toward me,
I mean."

"What do you expect?" Sandra asked, not looking
away from her mirror, brushing her long hair over and
over again.

"What does that mean?" I demanded.

Sandra shrugged. "There's no difference between a
turncoat and a traitor," she said flatly.

"What?"

"You know what I mean," she announced, putting
her brush into her purse and not looking at me.

"No, I don't," I said evenly. "I really and truly don't,
Sandra."

She shrugged again. "Sneaking around, taking notes
all the time," she said under her breath as though she
were afraid to be heard talking with me. "Telling the
newspapers what we're doing, what we think."

I was stunned. "I never once wrote about you."

"You could fool me," she replied. "What about that two-part piece that ran in the *Herald* last week?"

"What about it?"

"You don't think I recognized myself in *that?*"

"I didn't write that," I said hotly.

"Well, Ava, I simply don't know this Susan Woods. So, I ask you, who else writes for a newspaper?"

"You think I'm a spy?"

"Me, and a lot of other people."

And with that she picked up her purse and walked away.

The more I thought about it, the more stupid I felt. I guess I'd been so wrapped up in what Georgia was doing, and in what I was trying to do—stay behind the lines, help out anonymously, supply information and data—that I hadn't ever once thought about the *people* involved. I hadn't even noticed the kinds of things I began to see after that talk with Sandra. Actually, I had never written anything about her for the *Herald,* or given her name to Susan Woods, or even considered her anything more than a bystander. Which just goes to show the ego of some people.

Not that I was ostracized. In a way, I couldn't be. I was a senior and on the Student Council, and president of the Sharks. I mean, not to boast, but I did have some status around old Owanka High. What I failed to notice until then was that the hallways were getting progressively emptier and more quiet around me. No one pushed me around or actually threatened me. But I had never noticed before the number of people who slunk by with a smirk on their faces and said, "How's your sister?"

I wasn't mistreated, and I *could* understand what was happening, even though I didn't like it. Apart from the fact that sometimes what Susan Woods wrote in her newspaper was just about word for word what I wrote in mine, or that some of the people being quoted probably *could* identify themselves accurately, I *was* Georgia Van Buren's older sister. Guilt by association. Georgia was stirring up the town, the school, families, and friends by not lying quiet and letting adults organize her world. And if Georgia was liable to do that, why shouldn't I be suspect,too? If Georgia was sticking her cane in a beehive, wasn't it natural that I too was a troublemaker?

And, as a matter of fact, over the weeks I couldn't help but become more involved in what she was doing, especially since so much of it emanated from our very own house.

Georgia had become a wheeling, dealing, maddened field marshal during the final three weeks of the campaign. She had divided the city up into eight sectors and every afternoon dispatched her teams into its streets and walkways. If there hadn't been time for the kids her own age to get their assignments during the day at school, they automatically showed up at our house afterward to learn where they were being sent.

And it wasn't just kids, either. A lot of adults, mostly women but some men, too, came by and collected hand-outs and pamphlets and bumper stickers at three-thirty and went out onto the battlefield to do hand-to-hand combat with the forces of Repression and Evil. Some of these were library users, some not; some had kids in school, others had already sent theirs away to college or seen them married; some were retired and usually reticent about disturbing the peace. But with a cause and an election, they all worked together.

One afternoon, sticking to my journalistic belief that one had to interview and experience as much as possible, I decided that I, too, would hit the street for Georgia's team. I came home from school and found about a dozen people in our kitchen, milling about, waiting for their assignments, forming teams, making plans. (One of the consistently amazing things about all this was the authority of Georgia over this incredibly diverse group. I mean, she was leading and commanding and sending into fire people older than herself, people younger, people smarter and those less so, and no one ever challenged her or argued for more than a minute. Her word was gospel. Though I held back—feeling more comfortable in my journalistic pose—I *was* proud of her. Of course, I never said so. She would have thought I was talking down to her, or making fun, and I wouldn't have been. I guess sometimes no matter how much you'd like to give support to someone, you just can't for fear of somehow derailing them, distracting them, or splintering their concentration.)

While we were all waiting for Georgia, my mother provided hot chocolate and coffee to people, and cookies. There was never an afternoon when I saw her tire or grow short-tempered with the foot soldiers who slogged in and out. She asked supportive questions, greeted her friends warmly and their children with respect, made simple suggestions, and lent an air of encouragement to the troops always.

Anyway, I was talking then with Sally Ann Fickett, the Reverend Robert Fickett's youngest daughter, who was also a senior. Sally Ann is tall and perfectly blond, with a rosy complexion and bright eyes and a wonderful rolling laugh that has the effect of making anyone within earshot laugh too.

"Believe me," she was saying, "our family has seen worse fights."

"You have?" I asked, a little surprised. I mean, a minister's life is generally thought to be so calm, so trouble-free.

Sally Ann smiled knowingly. "It's not all ice cream and lollipops, Ava," she said. "We have problems just like anyone else. Of course, we carry an extra weight. And usually that extra is *your* problems, too."

"You mean people still actually go to their minister when they're confused or unhappy?"

She nodded. "Usually, of course, only when they've been everywhere else and tried everything they could think of. Then they come to my father and expect miracles."

"Which he can't provide," I supplied.

"Can anyone?" asked Charlotte Bracken, one of the few black girls in Owanka High and one of Georgia's most tireless campaigners. Rain or shine, windy or calm, weekdays or weekends, Charlotte showed up, her census forms under her arm and her pencils always sharpened, ready to go out and do battle.

"O.K.!" This was Georgia. "Enough of this idle chitchat, we've got work to do." She strode into the kitchen, dropping her books on the table there and scooping up a handful of Hershey's kisses Mother had put in a bowl for all her friends. The room quieted.

"Today we hit Sector Four," Georgia announced, drawing from her shoulder bag a sheaf of papers. "Charlotte, you go out with Mr. Wilson. Sally Ann's with Mrs. McCord. Ava—Ava? Are you gracing us with your presence for a reason?"

I blushed. "I thought I'd like to go along. Once."

Georgia nodded, all business. "Right, then. You can go with Mrs. Putnam and Eddy."

"Eddy" was Edward Lyon Tabott, the oldest in a family of six boys, all of whom until now had been thought retarded or at least confused. He wasn't bad-looking, just vacant. I had been surprised he was aboard Georgia's Freedom Train at all. I nodded at him and at Mrs. Putnam, a nice woman about thirty-five with two small pre-school kids of her own waiting for her out in her car.

There was little enough chitchat, as Georgia says, after the assignments were given out. Clearly Georgia's plan was that one adult should accompany each younger person, so that doors that tended to be slammed in the faces of kids would stay open out of respect for someone older.

"Are you observing, or working?" Georgia asked me as I passed her on my way out to Mrs. Putnam's car.

"Observing," I said. "I thought it would make a good story."

Georgia nodded, clearly having expected that reply. "Don't screw anything up, that's all," she warned.

"I won't open my mouth," I promised. "I'll just stand by listening."

Georgia grinned. "We'll see."

I got into Mrs. Putnam's front seat and Eddy got in back with her two little children. Then we set off across town for Sector Four. The front seat was clear but the floor at my feet held an enormous box filled with bumper stickers, pamphlets, campaign buttons ("A Little Wine Is Good for the Soul"), questionnaires and pledge forms. Also, of course, sharpened pencils and a box full of change.

I won't catalogue each stop we made along our route. Two incidents sort of honestly describe what we ran into, and what sorts of things were likely to happen.

At one home, we parked and organized, and then I followed Mrs. Putnam and Eddy Tabott up the front walk to wait, standing to the side in order to listen and yet not intrude in their work. We rang a doorbell and after a few moments a pleasant-enough looking woman whom I didn't know came to the front door. She opened it and stood inside the screendoor, smiling nicely.

"Mrs. Fawcett?" asked Mrs. Putnam. The woman nodded. "We're out campaigning to keep a book called

*The Grapes of Wrath* on our high school's reading list. You've probably read something about all this in the *Herald?*"

Mrs. Fawcett nodded, still smiling.

Mrs. Putnam nodded in return. "We were hoping you would help support our cause, which is really the cause of freedom to read what people want, after all. We'd certainly appreciate your help, in one way or another. I'd like to ask you to campaign in the neighborhood for us."

Mrs. Fawcett's smile wavered. "I'm not much good soliciting," she admitted.

"No, just among your friends, actually," said Eddy Tabott then. "Sort of rev them up, inform them what's at stake."

"I imagine they know about as much as I do already," said Mrs. Fawcett.

"Well then, perhaps you'd care to help us in another way?" asked Mrs. Putnam. "We need funds to advertise and to get our message across to the voters of Owanka. For only a dollar you could have a bumper sticker, or for fifty cents a campaign button."

She reached into her handbag and brought both items out so that Mrs. Fawcett could see them. Mrs. Fawcett saw them. There was a moment of silence. "Well, I suppose," said Mrs. Fawcett at last, "I suppose I could take a sticker."

"That's wonderful," Mrs. Putnam said, trying to sound enthusiastic.

"If you wouldn't mind," Eddy suggested then, "you could also answer some questions for us, if you would."

"Oh no, I couldn't do that," Mrs. Fawcett said hurriedly. "Be right back."

She turned and ducked down her hallway toward her purse, I assumed. When she returned, she held out a dollar bill. But she didn't open the door. There was an awkward moment before she realized that money offered wasn't magical enough to go through solids. She laughed self-consciously and blushed and opened the screendoor just enough to slip out the bill, which Eddy took; in exchange, he squeezed her bumper sticker through the slit.

"We're having a rally, you know," Mrs. Putnam told her quickly, before Mrs. Fawcett could turn and run away. "The night before the election. We'd be thrilled if you'd come to it, and maybe bring your husband."

"Oh no, I couldn't do that," Mrs. Fawcett said again.

"Well, if you change your mind," Mrs. Putnam offered, "at least you'll see a few friendly faces."

Mrs. Fawcett smiled sort of idiotically at this, immobilized for some reason, and so finally Mrs. Putnam nodded a goodbye and turned to walk back down the front walk. We all got into her car.

"She'll never use the sticker," Eddy guessed.

"I know," Mrs. Putnam said rather sorrowfully. "Still, we got a dollar."

"That's not much," I commented.

"No, but if we got a dollar from every house, we'd be rolling," Mrs. Putnam said with a stiff-upper-lip smile, starting the car and gliding down the same street to stop before another house. Once again we got out and followed her up a front walk. I spied around the corner of the house, in the driveway, a battered green sedan on whose back bumper were the fluorescent words SQUASH GRAPES! I struggled for a second or two, wondering whether to mention the lion's den into which we three were walking. I decided against it. After all, miracles do happen.

Mrs. Putnam rang the doorbell, but it was Eddy Tabott who stood front and center as a middle-aged woman, wearing jeans and a halter top and sneakers,

came to the front door. "Yes?" she asked rather forbid-
dingly.

Eddy blushed. "Mrs. Raymond, we're neighbors from
just across town, and we're very interested in—"

But Mrs. Raymond was clearly used to door-to-door
salesmen. "I don't need any," she declared firmly.
"Sorry you wasted your time."

"But—" Eddy started to say.

Mrs. Putnam came to his rescue. "Mrs. Raymond,"
she said almost as strongly as Eddy was timid, "we're
not selling anything. We need your support."

Mrs. Raymond had turned away but hearing that
someone *needed* her caused her to turn again and to
stand inside her screen, waiting.

"You probably know," Mrs. Putnam continued, "about
the special ballot on November 4."

Mrs. Raymond nodded, unsmiling.

"Well, a great many people in Owanka feel that if
that should pass, we would be censoring the reading,
the lives of our children."

"Not mine," Mrs. Raymond snapped.

"Pardon me?" said Mrs. Putnam, though I'm certain
she heard clearly.

"Mine are grown, gone, flown the coop," Mrs. Raymond said.

"Oh, I see," Mrs. Putnam allowed. "Then for you it
would be a matter of principle more than anything
else."

Mrs. Raymond nodded. "It is," she said. "I think that
book's trash!"

"You do? Have you read it?"

"Don't need to," Mrs. Raymond replied. "From what
I hear, there's dirty words on every page. Now, I don't
care what kind of book it is, what kind of story, but
people just don't need to write dirty words."

"But don't you think, being a reasonable woman,"

Mrs. Putnam suggested, "that really to be fair you ought to look into it yourself?"

"Nope," Mrs. Raymond said quickly. "Me and Nick both agree. What's filth is filth. And as far as we can see, if you let people get away with putting that stuff out, you're just inviting ruin. This country's already on her knees. Our job's to get her back up again, standing tall."

"But surely," Mrs. Putnam persisted, "one of the things our country's based on is the innocence of the accused until and unless he's *proven* guilty. Doesn't that apply to books, too? Shouldn't you *want* to examine the evidence before deciding?"

"Maybe I should, maybe I shouldn't," Mrs. Raymond told us. "But people I trust a whole lot more than you seem to think it's bad stuff, and I'm happy enough to go along with them." She paused and looked keenly through the webbing of the screen, her eyes narrowing. "Where do you all live, anyway?" she asked. "You don't look familiar to me."

"Just across town," Eddy Tabott managed to get out.

Mrs. Raymond squinted around at me. "You sure you're not some outside...agitator?"

Mrs. Putnam smiled. "Believe us, we all live here in Owanka. Eddy and Ava go to Owanka High."

"What's your church?" demanded Mrs. Raymond then.

Mrs. Putnam laughed gently and told her what she wanted to know. Then she said quietly, "I guess there's not much point in asking you to support our cause, is there?"

"Nope," said Mrs. Raymond. "I don't guess there is. Better luck somewhere else."

She turned quickly away back into her own house, not closing the heavier oak door inside because of the day's heat.

"Well," Mrs. Putnam said to us as we turned to walk back to her car. "I believe that's called losing some."

I smiled, but Eddy did not. "It's meanness, is what it is," he said under his breath. "Just closed-mindedness. People don't understand."

"The problem is, Eddy," Mrs. Putnam explained, "that people understand as much as they want to and then they stop listening. After all, it's far easier to make up your mind quickly, even if you're later proven wrong, than it is to listen to everything and everyone and then try to make an intelligent decision."

So the days passed, committees roamed the streets, candidates sought support and listeners, and issues became less clear and more broad. Stevie Wonder gave us "Hotter Than July," and Rod Stewart chipped in with "Foolish Behavior." If one wanted, one could find omens and warnings everywhere, some clearer and more direct than others.

# 15.

"It is *not* the most important thing in the world, Martin," I argued one Friday night after a pep rally when Martin had swung by to pick me up for a short ride. We had hightailed it out to Mill Pond and parked, and other couples, breaking training for the night, were doing exactly what we were doing. Or what we were supposed to be doing. What I had *wanted* us to do. But Martin wasn't seeing things my way. Instead of reaching across the seat and pulling me toward him, he had shut off the ignition and sat silently a moment before turning to me to say, "You have a choice to make, Ava."

"I have made a choice," I said then. "I just don't feel I have to publicize it, is all."

"You do have to," he said quietly. "Otherwise, what good is it?"

"What good is it if I say anything anyway?" I countered. "I mean, I don't vote, so what's the difference?"

He smiled a little in the darkness. "You ever hear that old line about standing up to be counted?"

"Of course," I said.

"Well, that's what good it does. It shows people where you stand. For all you know, you might actually be able to influence someone who does vote."

"Not very likely," I said. "Look, my father knows

how he wants to vote, and he's not out ringing doorbells or signing petitions."

"So you assume no one knows what he thinks?"

"Well, how would they?"

"They do," Martin assured me. "It's my guess that about fifty per cent of my father's cohorts are vocal, and fifty are just a little nervous about feeling the way they do. No matter that they think they're right, they're also unhappy about it. After all, the issue's been made pretty clear. One side wins and steps on the people of the other. The other side wins, and no one's hurt. Your father's silence is probably as eloquent as someone else's anger."

"Martin," I sighed, "could we, just for a few minutes, stop thinking about this, stop *talking* about it? Couldn't you just look at me and smile and hold my hand or something?"

He did what I wanted and we sat a moment silently. "Are you that frightened?" he asked softly.

I nodded. "I don't know why," I said weakly. "But I am. I've never seen people so ready to explode. I always thought Owanka was different, safer."

"It will be again, if we win," Martin said.

"God, what an enormous if!"

"You know," Martin said, almost whispering, "I'm proud of what you've been writing."

"You are?" Suddenly I was near tears.

He nodded.

"Martin, would you kiss me?"

We kissed. I felt warmed and safe and certainly happier.

"You know," he whispered in my ear, "I have an idea."

"What?" I asked, thinking I knew exactly what he was going to say.

"Why don't you write one more piece for *The Hawk,*

almost an editorial? Come out strong and straightfor-
wardly and then stop writing until after the election.
Say you can no longer remain objective and unbiased.
Really sock it to 'em and see what happens. I bet you'd
swing a lot of kids into Georgia's camp."

I was so flabbergasted by what Martin was suggesting instead of what I'd imagined, I was speech-
less.

"Are you thinking about it?" he asked.

I pulled away from him and slid back over to my
side of the front seat. "No," I answered bitterly, "I am
not thinking about it. Apart from the fact that I think
it's a stupid idea, it means betraying the newspaper
code of ethics. You just don't pick sides, Martin. You
report as objectively as you can. That's my job, my
duty."

"You have a personal duty, Ava," he said.

"Not now, I don't," I said hotly. "Look, just take me
home, O.K.?"

He shrugged and sighed and started the car. We
drove a bit and he started to say something but I cut
him off. I was steaming! How could he be so insensitive
to what I was trying to do? How could he compliment
me the way he had and then dump on me in the next
breath?

We'd driven about two miles back toward town when
we both heard what sounded like an explosion, rather
muffled, off somewhere to our left, toward the river.
We slowed down and peered out the windows, and
within a few seconds we saw a red glow in the sky, not
a huge leaping flame but rather an almost house-sized
coal on the horizon, glowing. Martin turned the car in
that direction at the next corner and we drove anx-
iously toward the flickering silhouette.

We turned down Drew Lane and saw a crowd of
people standing in the street in front of a pretty, well-

kept white frame house. In the driveway was a burning
hulk of a car, still smoldering, smoke billowing up and
around and then out sideways toward the bystanders.
We drove closer and then Martin pulled his El Camino
to the curb.

"For God's sweet sakes!" he whispered under his
breath, stopping the car altogether and getting out
quickly.

I squinted through the windshield. I did not know
whose house it was, or whose car, but suddenly amid
the crush of people standing to one side, watching
expressionlessly, I saw black faces, and remembered
Charlotte Bracken.

I felt weak suddenly and I knew I was perspiring.
I watched as Martin approached the people near the
drive, spoke to some of them, and then turned to walk
back again toward me. He opened the car door and got
in, switching on the ignition and beginning to back
away slowly. "No one was hurt," he said quietly.
"They've called the Fire Department."

"Fat lot of good that will do!"

Martin looked over at me and then back, swinging
the car around so that we were headed home.

"Well there, smart ass!" I said through my teeth,
shaking as I spoke. "That's what happens when you
take a stand. Like it?"

"That's not true, Ava," he said softly.

"Tell that to Charlotte Bracken!"

"It could have happened to anyone," Martin said.

"You don't believe that, and neither do I!" I said
angrily, clutching the dashboard. "They were an easy
target! The simplest! The meanest!"

"Ava, we don't know that," Martin said soothingly.

"Oh yes, we do!" I shot back. "I know it! God knows

who will get it next! The Blooms, maybe, or Sarah Weinstein."

"Don't jump to conclusions," Martin said. "After all, the police will be called into this."

"You don't think police vote?" I screamed.

Then I vomited all over the front seat of Martin's El Camino.

And looking back, I have to admit that while I was horrified at what I had done, it also gave me not a little pleasure.

# 16.

The next morning I tried to ignore all the sounds of my family beginning to stir. Georgia slipped out of our bedroom almost at first light, who knew for what? I didn't even raise my head to ask. I heard my parents downstairs having breakfast before my father set off for a half day's work at his hardware store (Owanka High's football team has a *lot* of supporters). There was conversation, oddly hushed and rather curt, it sounded to me, but I didn't tune in. I lay in bed, eyes clenched, pillow hugged against my chest, trying to clear my mind of what I'd seen the night before.

There were so many conflicting ideas bumping around in there. There was no certainty—I could admit that *now*—that what had happened to the Brackens' car had anything at all to do with the battle over righteousness versus paganism, i.e., with *The Grapes of Wrath*. On the other hand, there was, to my knowledge, no other source of tension or conflict in Owanka, no sign that relations between races were fraying or tearing at their edges.

Certainly there was paranoia about. I was one of its victims. I immediately assumed the worst, instantly blaming Mr. Brady's followers for what had happened, indicting even our tiny police force as racists and bigots and secret KKK members.

But the strange thing was that I wasn't particularly curious that morning about who in fact had firebombed the Brackens' car. Nor, when I thought about it, was I surprised that it had even happened in our town. We see so many things like that on television that when finally something happens to someone you know, or to yourself, you can almost make yourself believe that of course, it was coming, it was your turn, this is the way life is. I've known this all along and should have expected it sooner.

But that's a rotten way to feel, allowing all the wicked and demented people of the world to do what they will whenever they want because that's what life contains. Tragedy comes to everyone sooner or later. But if you begin to feel this way, and to accept it as a given in your everyday routine, you become almost a lightning rod, attracting or even willing catastrophe.

I rolled over and buried my head beneath my pillow, telling myself that if I could fall asleep again for just one more hour, I would get up to face the world. But I knew, even as I made the promise, that I would constantly peer up from under the feathers to look at the clock on my bedside table, so I might as well get the day under way, no matter how it was going to turn out. So I did.

"Morning, darling," said my mother as I came into the kitchen. "Are you starving, or just nibbly?"

"Don't ask me to make decisions," I told her wearily.

My mother shrugged and smiled. "Well, the makings are available for whatever you want. The paper's right there, too."

I looked across the table and saw the front page of the weekend edition of the *Herald*. Not too suprisingly there was a photograph there of the Brackens' car, burned out and standing looking rather surprised and alone in their driveway. It made me begin to shake, so I reached across the table and upended the whole thing onto the floor.

"Well now," Mother asked, ignoring the pile of newsprint, "what's on your schedule for today?"

I shrugged. "I think I'm going to call Mrs. Beaman and tell her I can't work at Chez Elle any more." Even I was surprised to hear this.

"You are?" asked Mother. "Why?"

I honestly didn't know, and said so. "It just seems right now there are other things I ought to be doing."

"You'll miss the money," Mother said.

"Maybe I'll just take a leave of absence until the election's over."

My mother nodded as she began loading the dishwasher. "Well, perhaps you'd like to help Georgia and me today, then," she suggested without turning around.

"To do what?"

"We're collecting for tonight's auction."

"What auction?" Even to myself I sounded increasingly out of it.

"For the Brackens," Mother explained over her shoulder. "Georgia is organizing a benefit to raise money for a new car."

I shuddered. "God, doesn't she ever let up?"

My mother looked quickly over at me and then bent back over the sink. "I think Georgia's idea is grand," she said positively. "I'm pleased she came up with it, and we're all doing what we can to help."

"Even Daddy?"

"Of course, why not?" asked Mother.

I stared at my place mat. "Where is this auction going to be?"

"At the stadium," Mother said. "Right after the game this afternoon."

"Really?"

Mother nodded. "Miss McCandless is arranging for it," she said. "We're all scouring attics and basements, asking neighbors, looking high and low for decent things people would want to buy."

For some reason I was beginning to feel positively light-headed. I tried to force a slice of bread into my mouth. "Who did it?" I asked around its crust.

"No one is sure," said Mother.

"No wonderful terrorist organization has taken responsibility?" I said only half-jokingly.

"Darling, that isn't funny," said Mother. "Besides, this is Owanka, not Italy somewhere."

"You could fool me," I said morosely.

Mother poured a cup of coffee for herself and sat down beside me at the table. "You're really very upset by all this, aren't you?" she asked nicely.

I nodded.

"Well, of course, so am I," she admitted.

"But you're so calm," I objected.

Mother laughed softly. "Actually, I'm not. I'm ticking away inside. Your father knows that. He's half-terrified I'll explode somewhere publicly. And I might."

"But you seem so—so capable, so strong," I said.

"Not everyone can give way to hysteria," she said. "Besides, I really believe our side will win."

"You do?" I was stunned. "Even with everything going on in the country, even with the election?"

"Even now," she said. "America has never been short its share of sensible, decent people. I'm relying on them, I suppose, or on Owanka's fair share."

I shook my head. "You're sure, and Georgia's sure, and Daddy's just as convinced on his side. Someone's wrong here somewhere."

"You know, Ava," Mother said reflectively, "I never regretted dropping out of college to marry your father.

I never regretted *his* decision to come back home to help his folks get along. Even *now,* when being more articulate and organized and having a little political savvy might be helpful, I'm still glad I did what I did— had all of you, worked so hard to get us started in town. Every once in a while I wonder whether I should be out getting a job myself, or at least looking for work now that you're all grown and so able to look after yourselves. But I feel good about being a mother, about being a wife, and I know I'm just reacting to what I read and see. *You* are my work. This town is. Our family is. This whole proposition now is part of my life. I want to protect our freedoms, and I'm willing to fight for them in my own way. I'd never have been the go-getter Georgia is. As a matter of fact, she's thrown me for a loop. I'd never have expected her to be so committed."

"She is amazing," I said noncommittally.

"Actually, if I were younger, I think I'd probably be more like you, a little distant, a little more cautious."

"I'm beginning to think that's not such an all-fired wonderful way to be," I said.

"Well, what else can you do?" asked Mother gently. "I mean, it's only common sense to think first, act later. If you're not absolutely sure where right is, or what is right for you, what could you do that would work better than to retire a bit, think things through, so that when the clouds clear, you're ready and convinced and able?"

"But there's no passion in that!" I said suddenly. "There's no adventure, no excitement!"

"Yes, there is," said Mother. "Stop and think. What is more worthwhile than looking out at the world and helping make sense of it for other people? I mean, that's what all writers do, really. They take stock of the confusion and anger and unhappiness and joy of life, and they transcribe it for beginners, if you like. It's like learning to play the piano. Not everyone can sit down and play a concerto. Someone somewhere *has* to be John Thompson, the person who makes playing understandable and easy for others."

Mother smiled. "Gracious, how I do go on," she said, sipping her coffee and standing up. "There's still so much to do for tonight." She paused. "Will you help us, Ava?"

"Yes."

# 17.

You wouldn't believe the kinds of things we found to auction off. People donated things they had already bought and wrapped to give at Christmas to their families and friends. Businesses donated small appliances (my father chipped in with a blender, a waffle iron, and a hand jigsaw), gift certificates, jewelry, a month's free groceries. There were skis and golf clubs, even a brand-new snowmobile. Clothing and shoes and, from basements across town, antiques and mementos and working lamps and ottomans and scarves and fur-lined gloves and you name it.

The stands at the field for the football game were half full. The day was overcast and rather chilly, so that if you had a choice, chances are you stayed at home and listened to the game on the radio.

The afternoon wore on into shadowy half-light, and our team won its game. But the strange thing was that as time passed, as quarter ran into halftime and out again, the stands began *filling* instead of emptying. By the time the game was ended and the players had moved off to the sidelines, there were more people ready for the auction than had attended the game to cheer.

When the game ended, my mother's car and perhaps ten others drove onto the torn and muddied grass to

park, tailgates facing the bleachers. A small wooden
stage was erected on the far rim of the cinder track
that circled the field itself, and microphones were
hooked up. Miss McCandless climbed onto the stage as
Georgia and some of her friends hoisted the items to
be sold onto the stage's apron so that people could get
a glimpse of the goodies.

"We're here this afternoon," Miss McCandless began,
"to show some friends of ours how we feel about them."
She smiled out into the stands and then, after a second,
continued. "Many of you have lived in Owanka far
longer than I, and I hope you won't be offended if I
speak for us all now. What happened last night was a
disgrace. It shamed us all, made us all smaller and less
human. We know that we cannot erase the shock and
trauma of that, but we want our friends to know that
most of us are feeling, sympathetic, caring human
beings, honest-to-God neighbors in the oldest and
truest sense, and that we are not only all lessened by
what happened, but also all responsible."

She stopped and seemed to smile rather hopefully
at one point in the crowd. I followed her glance, noticing
even as I did that Miss McCandless seemed nervous:
she was shaking just a little, and her color seemed
rather closer to crimson than was healthy. But there,
where she had focused for a second, were the Brackens:
not smiling, standing amid a sea of faces, Charlotte's
face showing the only animation, a cross between what
I would call a rueful grin and a frankly puzzled frown.

"Our auctioneer for this afternoon is Miss Georgia
Van Buren, whose hard work and dedication, indeed
whose very idea this event is. Georgia?"

Miss McCandless stepped aside and Georgia took her
place before the microphone. There was a small sound
of gloved hands clapping in the early evening air, and
she smiled blazingly. Then, typically, with no warm-

up, she lifted a golf bag full of a new set of woods and irons and began to make sounds that resembled an auctioneer's. Mother and I watched, stamping our feet occasionally against the damp ground, and we applauded and cheered when, after a few seconds, Georgia had secured a winning bid of seventy-five dollars. (Cheap, of course, but a start. After all, people need to be led along, urged, coaxed, they need to get in the spirit of things.) The next item, the month's "free" groceries, went for nearly two hundred dollars to a family large enough to have spent that much weekly. The crowd began to catch on.

Kids on the football team, who had not yet gone in to shower, moved among the crowd verifying bids, talking things up, joking and laughing and teasing people into a giving, holiday spirit. Martin did his share of this, smiling back at me every so often. I saw Sally Ann Fickett tower over one poor woman and nearly threaten her life if she didn't bid on the waffle iron. Louise Nichols took the microphone from Georgia to spell her at calling. Amos Allen made one of his rare appearances and bought the hand jigsaw for more than he would have paid to buy it in Father's store in the first place.

There was a curious sense of determination involved in this scene. People who bid and won items seemed almost to expect congratulations. Many of them were genuinely thrilled to have picked up a bargain, or at least to have purchased something at a reasonable price. But also many were the looks toward the Bracken family in the stands as the winning bidders climbed down from the bleachers to collect their purchases, looks over a shoulder or a thumbs-up sign that seemed to be pleading—if not for forgiveness, at least for understanding. Mr. Bracken stood stone-faced throughout the entire auction. His wife sat by his side, looking out, holding Charlotte's hand. Once in a while Charlotte would break and wave at someone, but that was the extent of their participation.

I don't think, if anyone had asked me, that I could have explained what Mr. Bracken must have been feeling. I couldn't even begin to guess. His posture was so straight, so firm and unforgiving, that as the sun went down and a real chill sliced across the field, it seemed to me he was a totem, a symbol, and that he knew it.

When the auction was over a total of fifty-six hundred dollars had been collected, not quite enough perhaps to buy the Brackens a replacement, but more than enough to help. Mr. Bracken climbed down from the bleachers as the people in the stands applauded, and mounted the small stage to take the microphone. There was an expectant, happy silence over the crowd.

"What's been done here this afternoon," he began in a low, deep, masculine voice, "has made you all feel better, and has reassured my family and me of the good wishes of you all. And we are grateful."

There was a long pause. Then a sort of half smile crossed Mr. Bracken's face and he seemed to catch the eye of his daughter.

"However," he said after a moment, "my family and I would prefer that the money you raised today, instead of being given to us, be donated to the Freedom Is Reading Is Freedom fund."

There was almost a collective intake of air in the crowd, a gigantic gasp. Then, after a few seconds, there was a tiny amount of applause. And then, without anything further being said, the stands began to empty and people drifted away from the field toward their homes and cars, walking in little clumps, round-shouldered, some red-faced, some smiling.

My mother and I packed up the few items we had collected that had not been sold, neither of us speaking. The Brackens walked across the grass in the direction of their home, arm in arm, alone, not surrounded any longer by faces or hearts. It was as though in one crazy but inspired action, Mr. Bracken had sliced the single rope that kept our small town's Ship of State at its mooring. We were all adrift.

# 18.

"Well, he was obviously upset," Robin said at dinner that night, having bussed down from Iowa City late that afternoon. "Besides, surely his insurance would have covered the car anyway."

"That's not the point," Georgia complained. "What we did, all of us, people who oppose Mr. Brady and people who support him, was respond as a whole town. It had nothing to do with politics. It was a *human* gesture."

"So you feel slapped in the face?" Robin suggested.

"Well, he was so...so stiff-necked!" Georgia said angrily.

"How can you criticize?" Robin asked her. "After all, what he did benefits *you*."

Georgia nodded, her face brightening. "I know and boy, we can sure use the loot! Not that we're greedy, you understand. But we can finally print brochures and flyers and maybe even get in an outside speaker for our final rally, and then—"

"Whoa!" said Father. "What final rally?"

Georgia blushed. "I thought you knew. I hoped everyone knew."

"Tell him," Robin coaxed.

"Well, on the night before the election, we're going to have a huge torchlight parade and then a rally in the square. Weather permitting, of course," she added.

"What's the point of that?" Father asked seriously. "Most people will have made up their minds by then."

Georgia shook her head vigorously. "Not at all," she reasoned. "If you read the same paper I do," and she grinned sheepishly, hearing herself, "you'll see a lot of people are undecided about the election itself, about Carter and Reagan. If they are, then here they're surely just as wishy-washy. A rally will show them that their instincts are right, that they're not alone. It will bolster us at the polls."

"It will?" Father sounded doubtful.

"I hope so, anyway," Georgia said. "I mean, I for one do not underestimate the opposition." She smiled at Father.

"You're going to lose," Johnny announced flatly then.

"What makes you so sure?" Georgia demanded.

"I just am, that's all," Johnny replied. "Everyone I know is against you."

"Is that so?" Georgia began to redden. "Well, just how many of your dimwitted little friends can even read, let alone vote?"

"The same question might be asked, darling, of your friends," Father said slowly.

"We don't expect to vote!" Georgia shouted. "What we're trying to do is educate the voters, help them see the issues, understand what's at stake! If we can do that, we have to win!"

"That's a big if," Father said.

Georgia sat very straight in her chair and stared at him. *"Life* is a big if," she said with dignity.

Robin laughed and tousled Georgia's hair and got up to begin clearing the table.

"You know, Jonathan," Georgia said then, "everyone has to learn to think for himself. You can't just rely on other people to make decisions."

"What are you talking about?" Jonny asked in return.

Georgia blushed but seemed committed. "I mean, just because Daddy feels a certain way is no reason you have to automatically feel the same."

"Now, Georgia," Mother said, "I don't really think—"

"Why not?" Jonny demanded. "He's never been wrong before."

"It's nice you feel that way, but not very sensible," Georgia pronounced. "This all affects you more than it does Daddy, you know. It's you who gets to read or not. Think about that for a while."

"I don't have to," Jonny said hotly, getting up from his chair. "I know what's right."

"You know what you've been taught," Georgia said quietly.

"Well, you've been taught the same things!" Jonny argued from his place at the table. "If *you* stopped to think, you'd agree with Dad!" And he turned quickly to leave the room.

"That seemed unnecessary," Mother said under her breath.

"Well, it's true, what I said," Georgia defended. "Just because he worships someone doesn't always make that someone right."

"Georgia, my love," Father said then, "if you have a quarrel to pick with me, why not just do it directly?"

"Because you won't listen to me!" she said quickly. "You're as bad as Mr. Brady. Your mind's already made up and that's that. Nothing I say or anyone else can make a difference!"

"That shouldn't keep you from trying," Father said.

"Well, it doesn't," Georgia answered. "It just makes one feel so useless. I mean, Jonny has a point, you know. We've all—Robin, too, even Rick—been brought up the same way, taught to believe in the same things. We *should* all see the same threat. And yet, there you sit, smug as a bug, determined to vote against me."

Father smiled. "I'm not voting against you, Georgia. I'm voting against an entire trend in American life of which I do not approve. This, after all, is a chance for me to register my feelings."

"That's so shortsighted!" Georgia argued as Robin returned from the kitchen to listen, standing behind her chair. "Don't you see, you can't stop publishers from putting out books. I mean, O.K., let's admit for a minute there are dirty words in this one. So what? If one publisher didn't print it, another would. You're not stopping anything except the freedom of us to read what we want. And if we want to read garbage, who cares? What I read doesn't harm you, does it?"

"The question is, darling, whether it harms you," said Father.

"Well, it doesn't," Georgia said firmly. "It certainly would not."

"It's not television, Dad," Robin said. "I mean, kids who watch a program that's violent sometimes *might* go out and copy what they've seen. But people read because they want to know about other lives, other times. *They* don't go out to act on what they've read. They might experience violence and degradation or whatever, but they've also been instructed about the price to be paid for living that way. I think writers are extremely moral, most of them. Most writers want to say something, to have their opinions registered and counted. That's what's at stake here. The freedom we all have to choose people to listen to, to learn from."

"That's a fine, academic point of view," Father said evenly. "But it doesn't address what concerns me."

"Which is?" Robin prompted.

"The way I see it," Father explained, "books that use unnecessarily rough language, films that dwell on violence, television news that glorifies criminals instead of making examples of them—they're all part of the same thing, a weakening of our spirit, of our good sense, our strength. I don't like it. I want to stand up, morally and with assurance, and say enough, stop, let's remember where we started and why. Let's try to keep our country closer to those ideals. Let's stop this slide."

"Admirable," Robin judged. "And much of what you say we all feel. But what you're asking us to do is give up our freedom because some people have abused it."

"Robin's right, Fred," Mother said. We turned to look at her. "Because there are bad apples, we don't do away with the crop. We weed more carefully, select carefully, pick and choose. But what you're saying is that we have to stop growing apples altogether, and that isn't fair, not to us who thrive on them."

"I'm not saying you, Alva, aren't capable of making good selections," Father said. "What I'm saying is that there are children and young people with less experience who cannot be expected to understand what's fitting and proper."

Mother smiled softly. "What you do to the least of them, you also do unto me," she paraphrased.

"You're not seriously trying to tell me," Father asked, "that you think Georgia and people her age have as much maturity and understanding of the world as you and I?"

"No, I'm not," Mother agreed. "But I am saying that what you advocate only manages to keep them ignorant, it doesn't in the long run make them any more capable of making decisions you can approve."

"How do people learn to separate good from evil?" Robin said. "If we have no experience of evil, how do we recognize it? How can we choose if we have no experience? What kind of parents will Georgia and her friends be if they're not allowed to learn about the world, all of it, the good and the bad?"

"Unfortunately," Father said, standing up from his chair and clearly ready to end the discussion, "there is more than enough of both out there, good and bad. Exposing people to less of the bad is only a beginning."

"Fred, you can't mean that," Mother said, standing at her place, too, as Father came round the table. "I mean, that's perilously close to advocating a benevolent dictatorship."

But Father wouldn't argue the point. He kissed her quickly on the cheek and put his arm over her shoulder. "Come on, sweetheart, let's take the kids on at Scrabble."

*Scrabble!* I shrieked to myself. *Talk about fiddling while Rome burns!*

"You're very quiet tonight," Robin said as I helped clear the rest of the table.

I nodded. "I'm having a confidence crisis."

"Over what?"

"Very funny," I said, smiling. "Over life."

Robin laughed.

"I'm serious," I protested. "All around me people feel passionately about something. I keep waiting for my own emotions to reach their boiling point, but all they do is simmer."

"At least there's a fire on."

I smiled. "The trouble is, Robin, I can understand Daddy's point of view. I can see where Mother's coming from. I appreciate Georgia's stand. Somehow everyone has been able to tie into this thing. It means different things to them all but they're all committed. What's the matter with me?"

"Maybe you're afraid of being alone for a while," Robin said thoughtfully.

"What do you mean?"

"Well, that's what happens sometimes when people take stands. They find themselves deserted, stranded in the middle of life with only themselves for support. You have to be pretty strong, pretty sure of yourself to be able to handle that."

"Well, how in hell can someone like Georgia, who's only fourteen, for heaven's sakes, be that secure?"

Robin shook his head. "It hits people at different times, I guess."

"I have as much resource as other people," I said then.

"Fine," he agreed. "Then use it. Don't be afraid of it. Why do you think Georgia hooked you into that girl, what's her name, Susan—"

"Susan Woods?" I asked. I was astounded. "How do you mean, Georgia hooked me into her?" I was terrified of his answer.

Robin grinned. "Well," he said, "Georgia thought you were sitting in a fairly powerful spot, what with your work for *The Hawk* and all. And she didn't think you recognized how much you could do to help the cause."

"It wasn't *my* cause!"

"Still and all, Ave, you know Georgia—straight ahead, damn the torpedoes, whatever. She told Susan Woods she thought you'd be interested in working for a real newspaper, and since you were at O. High to begin with, Georgia understood the *quid pro quo*."

"The what?"

"Tit for tat, back scratching. There's a good reason for you to expand, to punch up your chances for college, to bear down and make a good record. And there's a good reason for Susan Woods to be interested in you because of your sources at school, because you have lines out that she doesn't. Georgia put it all together and discovered she could push you a little at the same time she helped her own crusade."

I shook my head. "Darryl was right," I muttered.

"What?"

I smiled unhappily. "The night Susan Woods came over to ask me to work with her, a friend of mine was here, Darryl von Vrock. He saw through her instantly. He even told me. I was so flattered at being asked to help out of the blue like that I never even saw it."

"It hasn't done you any harm, has it?" Robin asked with a gentle smile.

"No," I admitted. "It's been fun, valuable, I suppose. I've learned things."

"Well, there you are," he said happily. "Georgia got you involved. You learned more about newspapers and writing. Susan Woods got a news stringer. I'd say it all worked out for the best"

"Then how come I don't feel better about it?"

Robin shrugged and poured detergent into the dishwasher. "Maybe it's what you said before. You're just having a crisis, that's all."

I leaned back against the sinkboard, feeling oddly brighter for a moment. "Does it seem too selfish," I asked, "to have a small, *personal* crisis when all around me other people are having bigger ones?"

"No," Robin answered, straightening up. "I'd say that's a good sign, as a matter of fact. It means you haven't been inoculated yet, that you're still vulnerable. Good for you. Stay that way."

# 19.

The next morning, before church and after breakfast, we all sat down in the den to watch "Newsmakers," a program that was televised in Des Moines, the state capital. The grapevine—as well as our local edition of *TV Guide*—had told us who the program's guests were going to be: Joel Claffin, the tenth-grade teacher in whose classes *The Grapes of Wrath* were theoretically tasted; Laura McCandless, the librarian from Owanka High; Stanley Sopwith; and Mrs. George Nichols.

It's strange watching people you know on television, sitting there discussing matters and personalities you yourself are so well acquainted with that you always want to interrupt and correct them.

There were two particular moments I recall from this program. In one, Joel Claffin was trying, in his usual laid-back, gentle, afraid-to-give-offense manner, to explain how he felt about the entire battle. "It's so multifaceted," he said. "The freedom to read has become mixed up with God and abortions and foreign policy and inflation. I think people are striking out in frustration. If the times we lived in were better for America, I doubt very much whether we would be facing this choice at all."

Miss McCandless disagreed. "I'd have to argue that,"

she said quickly. "There are always manipulators, people out for power. If you can frighten enough other people, cause them to rely on only you, you can be king of the whole world. What we have in Owanka is a town full of the blind. And a one-eyed man."

Jonny looked up at Father to ask what Miss Mc-Candless meant. "In the city of the blind, the one-eyed man is king," Father explained, smiling in his lopsided fashion. Jonny reflected a moment and then laughed, got up, and went back upstairs to finish dressing for church.

Miss McCandless was beginning to get up a full head of steam. She sat, fidgeting and almost quaking, for another few seconds of small talk between the program's moderator and Louise Nichols, and then she burst.

"Mrs. Nichols is being too kind," she said. "What we're faced with in Owanka is one man's ambition, and the concurrent stupidity of the rest of the town!"

She took a big breath. "This book is not harmful. It's a classic. But to read it is just too much for our citizenry; certainly for most of them. They'd far rather listen to their friends who—also never having read the thing—believe what they've been told by politicians with axes to grind or, rather, with goals that have little or nothing to do with what most Americans think of as freedom."

"The freedom to protect our children is something we *all* treasure," Stanley Sopwith broke in.

Miss McCandless laughed sharply, her image on the screen becoming almost angular. "And what about protecting the rest of us, *Mr.* Sopwith?" she demanded. "Are *you* getting threatening telephone calls offering to burn down *your* house? Is there hate mail waiting for *you* at the end of *your* hard day's work? Is garbage dumped on *your* lawn while you're sleeping?"

I gasped. So did Mother. We'd had no idea that sort

of thing was happening, even though Mr. Claffin had alluded, in his own way, to the same sorts of pressures. Suddenly I wondered why *we,* or rather *Georgia's family,* weren't being hit by the same barrage of intimidation. The only reason I could see would be that Owanka is a small town, after all, and people must have learned about Father's feelings and decision. That might counter Georgia's own angry and insistent drive.

"Are you implying," Stanley Sopwith said, getting even redder than Miss McCandless, "that Mr. Brady and I are hooligans?"

"Listen," Miss McCandless cut in, "I can put up with that kind of harassment. I shouldn't have to, but I can. And I'm not saying you or Mr. Brady or anyone is directly responsible, just that I thought this sort of election tactic had passed with the Chicago of the thirties."

She leaned forward, closer than before to Stanley. "What I *am* saying is that your side is trying to protect an image of life as you want it to be, not life as it *is.* Adults get nervous around honesty and guts, and they want their kids equally timid. And if kids aren't free to learn about the world in which they're expected to operate as they grow, well, of course, they'll be just as frightened and blinded as their parents!"

"Time for church," Father said suddenly, standing up to switch off the television set.

"Daddy!" wailed Georgia. "How can you? That's the most important thing that's ever happened to Owan—"

My father frowned and cleared his throat. "Thanking our Creator for His blessings ranks a good bit higher than that show, Georgia."

There was no point in arguing and Georgia knew it.

Church services, as you can imagine, were not a barrel of laughs that Sunday. It seemed that most of the congregation had been tuned to WHO-TV along with us, and there was a frantic and constant buzz throughout most of the morning.

I paid attention to what people were saying as we filed out later, listening to people argue or support one position or the other, warming up their speaking voices for the vote that would be taken the following week. Since Mr. Fickett's church had voted to support him and his letter to the *Owanka Herald,* all churches in Owanka seemed to feel they, too, had to step forward to be counted. I had the distinct impression that that morning's television interview had solidified some wavering minds.

We got home in fairly good time; the weather had improved and warmed a bit, and walking back to the house was rather a treat, almost a family outing with Robin on hand, lagging just behind the rest of us with Jonny in tow, pointing out signs of winter that nature was sprinkling along our trail—a sort of reverse breadcrumb theory.

We had finished our Sunday meal—a pork roast and apple sauce, with green beans and sliced tomatoes and freshly baked bread—when the front door opened and we heard someone enter the house. We all looked expectantly at the threshold of the dining room and there, looking as though he hadn't slept in weeks, or shaved since Easter, was Rick.

He stood a moment looking at us one by one, and then he smiled tiredly. The effect was unreal. He looked so thin and tired that when his face creased, it seemed to be breaking apart. "God, it's good to see something so normal," he sighed, and drew up a chair near Mother's place.

"Is anything wrong at school?" asked Father.

"No, I just needed a little comfort," Rick said, looking sideways at Robin. "I needed to come home and check in, sort of."

"What about the *specialité de la maison?*" Mother suggested brightly, standing then and putting her hand on Rick's shoulder. "Marble cake and chocolate ice cream. You want yours with chocolate syrup or plain?"

"Load it up," Rick answered with as much enthusiasm as he could muster. "You need help?"

"Ava can help me," Mother said. So, dutifully but puzzled, I stood up and helped remove the plates from the table and serve the dessert. Mother brought in the coffee pot and then, through the strange and rather thickened air of tension in the room, Georgia proceeded to bring Rick up to date on developments in the Brady affair. He listened and asked appropriate questions, giving Georgia half-attentive encouragement, but clearly his mind was elsewhere, waiting to get himself together with Robin to explain to him, if not to the rest of us, his sudden arrival.

Father decided to take Jonny out to the river for some lazy Sunday afternoon angling. Mother put some marble cake in aluminum foil for the two of them and marched them off while Georgia excused herself to work upstairs on her notes for her rally appearance. When Mother returned, she edged me back into the kitchen with her, leaving Rick and Robin to sit alone at the dining-room table, nursing their coffees.

Mother and I worked fairly quietly in the kitchen, purposely keeping noise to a minimum so the guys could get down to settling whatever it was that needed settling. *My* understanding of what was said in the dining-room was necessarily piecemeal, what with the running of hot water and scouring of pans and pots, and then the dishwasher being turned on, the garbage disposal, the regular symphony of middle America going about its chores.

Robin: "Judging from your phone call and the look

on your face, it doesn't seem as though you've solved your problem."

Rick: "The vines keep growing, no matter how hard I hack away at them. Every time I think I've come to a decision, I think of some other consideration, and end up having to start deciding all over again."

Robin: "That's better than going off half-cocked."

Rick: "I'm not sure. At least I'd be *going,* I'd have decided."

Robin smiled (I could tell by the tone in his voice): "You underrate yourself, kid. I mean, you've been going and coming now for weeks."

Rick: "Very funny."

Robin: "But I'm serious. If you didn't call me every time you felt at sea, you'd probably have made a decision by now you could live with."

Rick: "I think I have."

Robin: "You *think?*"

Rick: "Well, I thought so, when I left this morning. Now I'm not so sure."

Robin: "Where was your head when you got in your car?"

Rick: "I'd made up my mind to drop out after the end of the first semester."

Robin: "And now?"

Rick: "Now, I look at Father and feel guilty and rotten and decide I should stick it out, at least till the end of the year."

Robin: "Are you any closer to knowing what you'd do if you did drop out?"

Rick: "No. Maybe get a job. Maybe go into the Army. Just find something to do for a while until college either seems more worthwhile to me, or doesn't. I can't *be* there and think about it at the same time."

Robin waited a moment. "You know, in my psychology course we're learning about what used to be called 'sensitivity training.' All that means is finding out how to get people to do what you want to without making them feel silly or used. You build them up, flatter them, and then slip the message in." He laughed quietly. "Like this. 'You know, Rick, you're an incredibly bright guy. You've got all the natural ability of a great athlete, you're popular and friendly, you're a lady-killer, you're just an incredibly insightful human being. So what I can't understand—'" and here Robin began laughing in advance "'—is how you can be so darned stupid about a little thing like college.'"

Rick (laughing obligingly): "That's a cute approach, cute. But it doesn't make me feel any better."

Robin: "It's not supposed to. What it's designed to do is make you reconsider, think again. That's all I'm suggesting."

Mother heard their laughter, too, although the look on her face was anything but lighthearted. She turned on the faucet, shaking her head. "Things are so much more complicated now than when I was that age," she said sadly. "This will hurt your father deeply."

"It shouldn't," I said. "After all, it's Rick's life."

"No, Ava," Mother said. "You see, both your father and I left college before we graduated. Rick and Robin are our second chance; you all are. I don't see how anyone, especially now, with all that's going on around us, can even begin to doubt the value of education."

"I don't think Rick does," I argued quietly, since the boys could probably hear us if we could hear them. "He just doubts its timing."

"I hope you're right," Mother said.

So did I. Even though, in my heart of hearts, if anyone had asked me, I would have said that not everyone in the whole world benefits from going away to school.

"The crazy thing is," we heard Rick say then, "is that I agree with Father about this *Grapes of Wrath* thing.

I mean, if I see eye to eye with him on that, why can't I agree with him about staying in school?"

Robin: "For God's sake, don't say anything to Georgia. She'll be brokenhearted."

Rick: "Just because someone disagrees with her? That's not very sensible."

Robin: "Just at this very moment, at this point in time, as people say, Georgia doesn't happen to be sensible about a lot of things. She's too wrapped up, too involved. Although, if you'll allow me to carry her standard into battle, I think you're crazy!"

# 20.

If one had drawn a graph of community spirit during this period, I think its highest point would have been the auction for the Brackens—up until the moment when Mr. Bracken donated the proceeds to FIRIF. From then on, as the saying goes, it was downhill all the way.

That Monday began a period of leveling, of seeing where people stood, waiting to see what would happen next. Kids at school seemed rather subdued. Some few got a kick out of the limelight or at least being on its outer fringes, and flattered Georgia and teased her good-naturedly. Others, the enemy finally identified, cut her in the halls and confused her.

As for me, I was trying hard to come up with one final riveting idea for *The Hawk* on the entire *Grapes of Wrath* affair. Not that I was willing to say my piece and move offstage. But it seemed to me that more than enough was already being said and written about us all, and what was needed was a simple, short article that tried to put things into a clean, clear focus, something personal and yet brief, meaningful and yet, if possible, distant, measured, sensible.

What I was looking for was handed to me almost on a platter the next day, for on Monday, at a specially called City Council meeting, it was announced that

Miss Laura McCandless had resigned as librarian at
Owanka High School.

Susan Woods had somehow got wind of this event
before it was publicly revealed, and in the *Herald* the
next morning was an interview, short but to the point.

## LIBRARIAN DISMISSED

### McCandless Forced to Resign

#### By SUSAN WOODS

OWANKA, Oct. 27.—It was announced last night at the Owanka City
Council meeting that the librarian of
Owanka High School, Ms. Laura
McCandless, an outspoken supporter
of FIRIF (Freedom Is Reading Is Freedom) and opponent of the November
4th ballot issue concerning *The Grapes
of Wrath,* has resigned her post, effec-
tive immediately.

Reached by telephone later, Ms.
McCandless viewed her resignation in
this way.

"I was asked to resign," she told me.
"Apparently some remarks made Sunday on WHO-TV were felt offensive by
some of the Council members. I want
people to know that I was firmly supported by Mrs. Louise Nichols, chairperson of the School Board Committee. And also that I was dismissed not
for any dereliction of duty or work
deficiency, but purely for personal
conviction."

> **Mr. Fairchild Brady, president of
> the City Council, would make no state-
> ment other than to say that a source
> of "divisiveness within the educa-
> tional community has been capped."**

I was stunned.

All day Tuesday, during classes and during breaks,
I tried to find something to say that would carry how
I felt, how I thought a lot of people would feel. But I
couldn't find the right beginning, or the right ending,
or the words that once begun would flow and fill my
notepad and then my typewriter. I wanted something
angry, something American, something emotional but
reasonable. And all day I came up dry.

I had promised to go to the movies that night with
Darryl von Vrock. Our enterprising local movie theater
manager had obtained a print of the film of *The Grapes
of Wrath* and had hustled it into the Varsity for one
week only. There was no way out as far as I could see,
and if I said I had a cold or the flu, the next day I *would*
have it and I wasn't about to take that chance. Besides,
what harm could come from just going to the movies
with Darryl?

(To be frank, I knew exactly what harm could come.
It meant skirmishing in the dark, one eye on the screen
and the other on Darryl's speedy right hand, or left, as
the case may be. Not that one doesn't expect attempts
at little liberties along one's path. But a movie theater
is a public place and if I feel inclined to grant a few
insignificant signs of affection to someone, it certainly
isn't about to happen while I'm surrounded by friends
or, worse, rivals.)

Not that I wasn't pleased enough to go out with Darryl. But I had begun to find the distance he kept from
what was happening all around him uncomfortable. I

didn't feel it was loyal or even grown-up not to be involved at *some* level.

The theater was nearly full for the seven o'clock show. The crowd was attentive and well behaved, and people seemed scarcely to breathe during the movie, so intent were they on hearing every word. I was among them, despite the fact that I knew how the story ended, what was coming, what was going to happen. Which, as it turned out, was a good thing, because the distraction of Darryl on my left was considerable. He seemed made of rubber. His hands came at me from all directions. The lights in the Varsity dimmed and I was under attack.

"Stop it!" I whispered at him.

"What, stop what?" He grinned at me.

"Oh, come on, Darryl, you know," I complained. "Besides, I warned you."

His arm shifted. Ten seconds later, another arm appeared on my shoulder. "Darryl!"

"Shhh!" someone said a few seats away.

"We're too old for this," I said to him under my breath. "Come on, we're not kids."

"I don't feel too old," he said in return. "I won't ever feel that old."

I lifted his hand and placed it on his lap, atop his other hand. "There, isn't that better?" I asked sweetly.

"Than what?" he asked.

"Than getting slapped?" I shot at him.

This seemed to have some effect.

We settled in to watch the action on the screen, which centered around Henry Fonda as young Tom Joad, and on Jane Darwell, who played his mother. It was sad and sobering to watch poor people pushed off their land and forced to flee virtually across an entire continent just on hope, with no money, not enough food,

no water to bathe in or to drink, no jobs along the way
to help pay for lodging and a little comfort. Even Darryl
was finally enthralled by the film and sat well behaved,
staring at the screen.

When the lights came up on the audience, you could
see handkerchiefs in some people's hands and sense the
sadness the story had left them with. We all filed out
of the theater in almost total silence, and very few
people hung around outside talking.

"I don't think this is going to work to your advan-
tage," Darryl said to me as we got into his car.

"What do you mean?"

"Well, I think it was a good idea to bring the movie
in," he said, closing his door and starting the ignition.
"But did you notice? There were hardly any bad words
used. There really wasn't anything that was horrible
or traumatic or seedy up there on the screen."

"But that's good!" I objected. "I mean, for all the
people who haven't read the book to see there's nothing
to be afraid of."

Darryl shook his head and grinned sideways at me,
rather slyly. I didn't much like the look.

"You really don't understand how this life works, do
you?" he asked. "Can't you see what will happen? If a
whole movie, if millions of dollars were spent bringing
the book to the screen and not one single word or scene
was objectionable or lurid, that's just more ammunition
for Mr. Brady."

"I cannot understand what you're saying, Darryl,"
I admitted just a little tartly.

"If the story could be told without swear words and
dirty things happening in the movie, then it could certainly have been told the same way on the printed
page," Darryl explained. "Brady will just say that if
Steinbeck *had* to write this book, this is the way he
should have done it."

"That's Monday morning quarterbacking," I said.

"So what?" Darryl asked. "It makes a certain amount of sense, doesn't it? Besides, with the movie here in town, people don't have to read the whole book for themselves to make up their minds. This is the way they'll get acquainted with it."

"I think that's hateful!" I announced. "Not just what you say, which may happen, who knows? But that you can even think so crookedly!"

"I'm only trying to think the way Brady and his gang will," Darryl defended. "In a fight like this, you have to try to outguess your opponents. This is grown-up life, after all, Ava. There's nothing fair about it."

"Well, there should certainly still be some rules."

"If there were, Brady wouldn't have pushed McCandless into quitting. He wouldn't have had the clout to do it."

We were parking in my driveway then. I looked at my house, all lit up and friendly and comforting, and I couldn't wait to get inside. More, I didn't think I much cared for Darryl's instinctive ability to think the way the opposition did. At all.

"Darryl," I said then, "I hope you won't be offended by what I'm about to say."

"I won't know till I hear it, will I?" he said confidently.

I smiled, a little wickedly I hoped. "Darryl, you may be right about how you see the world. I'm perfectly willing to admit you've seen more of it than I have. But I don't like your view of it very much." I took a deep breath. Why stop now? "And I don't really, down deep, like you very much, either."

There was a moment of silence in the car. "No one is forcing you to go out with me, Ava," Darryl said

irmly. "It's all the same to me. If it wasn't you, it would
be somebody else."

I winced a little and hoped that in the darkness he
couldn't see.

"This whole town is living in the nineteenth cen-
tury," Darryl continued. "I can't wait to get to college,
to get out into the real world to meet people who know
what life is all about."

"Well," I said, opening my own door, "I sure hope
there *is* a real world out there waiting for you. Especially one filled with people who are as sophisticated
and cynical as you think." I got out of the car and leaned
quickly back in. "Thanks for the movie, anyway."

"Yeah," Darryl said, sounding surprisingly sad, I
thought, or maybe that was just what I hoped I heard.

I bounced into the house, walking right past my parents and heading directly upstairs. I liked the rules of
the game, as *I* understood them, not as Darryl did. I
sat down at my desk and began to write my Thursday
morning piece for *The Hawk*.

# 21.

## Owanka, and the Eighteenth Century

Anyone who thinks that the current uproar over *The Grapes of Wrath* is not a matter of personal freedom this week should think again.

Because Miss Laura McCandless, librarian here at O. High, chose to exercise her constitutional rights of free speech, of viewing life in a different manner, of lobbying for her point of view, she was forced to resign.

The United States of America was founded by men clear-sighted enough to remember what had brought settlers to these shores originally: dissent, the desire to be free of other people's rules and regulations.

That some of Miss McCandless' opinions angered certain august citizens of Owanka is clear. What is even clearer is that she is being deprived of

her right to earn a living as a free citizen in a democracy *because* she chose
to believe in those rights, for all, including herself.

The separate ballot measure is not
simply a matter of protecting Owanka's
(ultimately unprotectable) youth from
unsuitable literature and language.

It is the first step toward regulating
how we all must learn to think and to
feel and, finally, to conform to the
rules of behavior advocated by a small,
vocal, and frightened group of people
who have forgotten, or are ignoring,
the precepts upon which this country
was founded.

We sincerely hope that Miss Mc-
Candless will stay in Owanka and continue to fight for what she feels is
right.

And anyone who votes on November 4th to curtail *her* freedoms, or
*mine,* or *yours,* stands accused herein
of betraying our unique and treasured
American way of life.

                              Ava Van Buren

# 22.

I think that the resignation/firing of Miss Mc-
Candless gave everyone on Georgia's side hope. The
unreason of Fairchild Brady and his determination to
win at any cost was exposed, and his opponents for the
City Council hammered relentlessly at him for forcing
the issue. Mr. Brady, for his part, tried to keep sailing
as he had before, calmly, rarely raising his voice, doing
his best to disarm his enemies by repeating his argument that taxpayers' dollars should not finance cor-
ruption and immorality in the city's young people.

My own campaign stand seemed to have been noticed
with nothing but silence. Kids in the halls treated me
as they had been doing—either they were friendly, if
they agreed with me, or they were silent, if they didn't.
No teacher made comment; no grades were raised; no
duties were lifted from my shoulders. I began to think
the piece in *The Hawk* had been printed in my imagination only. I felt as though I were in a crowded room
and had said something particularly brilliant, but no
one had taken notice, and so I began to doubt I had
spoken at all.

The campaign was winding down, or up, as you like.
There were only two major events scheduled before the
election itself. The final rally, of course, and the deci-

sion of our church to stand on one side or the other, publicly, of the issue.

For a small town, Owanka seems very devout. We have twelve churches for just over six thousand people. By the time our church was ready to take its stand, others had already stood up and been counted. It will come as no surprise that Mr. Bracken's church (one of three Baptist congregations in town) supported FIRIF. On the other hand, the Catholics and Mrs. Louise Nichols' own Presbyterians came down on the opposite side.

It is difficult to describe that particular Sunday service. As I think back, not much seems to have been recorded in my mind in sequence. I *do* remember that the congregation sang "A Mighty Fortress Is Our God" with a new resolution, and, really, almost a sort of subterranean anger.

My mother sat ramrod straight during the entire service, between Jonny and Father, looking neither left nor right, her features frozen in something akin to dread. At first I was puzzled, but then I remembered the argument Georgia and I had heard from the porch, and I realized that what Mother was doing—almost literally—was holding her breath.

The pastor threw open the meeting to his parishioners, deferring for once a sermon. Everything happened so quickly and at such volume that I couldn't begin to identify all the speakers. I hadn't brought Martin's recorder. But this will give you an idea of how that morning service ran.

Man: "What makes you think your kids don't know those words already? Or worse? I mean, who are you protecting? Yourselves?"

Woman: "It's a matter of drawing a line. And as far as I can see, the public purse is as good a place as any to start."

Woman: "This has nothing to do with taxes. It has to do with letting children grow and learn. God knows, we have enough trouble making them study. If they want to read this book, I say let them."

Man: "That's an incredibly stupid attitude."

Woman: "Well, at least it's the way *I* feel, not some bunch of hypocrites a thousand miles away!"

Man: "What's hypocritical about wanting our children to grow into God-fearing, right-thinking citizens?"

Woman: "Besides, it's a chance to stop permissiveness and drugs and..."

Woman: "This is a matter of personal freedom. I wouldn't want my freedom voted on by other people!"

Man: "And are we ready to have the City Council come into our lives to tell us what to do and what not to? I'm certainly not!"

Man: "Yeah, well, it's liberals like you who cry over criminals and then turn around and want the death penalty reinstated."

Woman: "At least I'm not a right-wing bigot who cowers under white sheets!"

Man: "I'd rather have Fairchild Brady running the town than some smart-assed fourteen-year-old!"

"Let us pray!"

It was with nothing but relief that we all left the church finally, the secret ballot having been taken. No one really cared to stay another second in the angry heat of God's house just then, so we all gathered outside to wait to hear the final tally.

Which, when it came, caused even more anguish, for the congregation had voted narrowly to come down on the side that wanted the book banned from the tenth grade.

Arguments began all over again, right there on the leaf-strewn lawn, but we didn't stay. Following Mother's lead, we turned back toward our own house and walked slowly along the roadside.

Suddenly Mother halted and stood beneath an emptying cottonwood tree, waiting for the rest of us to catch up. When we did so, she put her arm over Jonny's shoulder and drew him in toward her body and looked at Georgia and me with tear-filled eyes.

"I have a confession to make," she said haltingly, unsteadily.

We waited.

"I'm just as bad as Fairchild Brady," she said quietly. "I made your father promise not to speak out at church today. I threatened him. In fact, what I did was censor his right to speak and be heard. And I am terribly ashamed of myself."

She bent her head and tears appeared on her cheeks. I didn't know what to do, and neither did Georgia. We both just stood there, our wrists hanging out of our coats, aware of the wind and the sound of Mother's weeping.

My father stepped quickly up to embrace her. He said nothing, just held her tenderly, patting her shoulders, kissing her hair.

After a minute, my mother's sobs softened and then stopped altogether, and she raised her eyes and looked up at Daddy. He smiled reassuringly, lovingly, still saying nothing, and then he turned her around toward home and we all followed silently.

# 23.

It was Martin Brady who pointed them out first—strangers. The whole place, day by day, was crawling with aliens carrying in what seemed foreshortened arms all kinds of electronic wizardry with which they were able, at a fraction of a second's notice, to record and transmit for posterity the most minute feelings and sensations of us earthlings in Owanka. Some came harnessed, some wore headdresses which were equipped with their own antennae and lamps, and with all the wires and cables it was clear they were attached, clinging, to some distant Mother Ship to which they could be recalled on the instant.

The Press.

Not just people like Susan Woods with notebook, pencil, and on a good day a photographer in tow. But people you thought you recognized from network newscasts, and probably did. And who do you suppose was the central focus of all this new attention? You guessed it.

Not that the rest of us were ignored. Almost as often as Georgia did her single, we did a backup group. That's really the way it came to seem. Georgia the star, and us behind her, slightly to one side, fingers clicking and knees bouncing flexibly, humming doo-wah or ohyeahs as she sang the verses. We got to meet Cassie McKay from ABC, Ed Bradley of CBS, Chris Wallace from NBC. Not to mention their local counterparts on stations in Des Moines and Chicago, Davenport and Kansas City. Anthony Lewis flew out from the *New York Times*. Mike Royko came in from Chicago. And *Newsweek* sent an entire team to cover the story.

Not that everything, every day, went swimmingly. The press did not see everything. There was one grand midnight battle between Georgia and Daddy over whether she should be allowed some new clothes to match her new role of Jeanne d'Arc. And there was a wonderful set-to between them over whether Father should be allowed to reveal his own stand on the issue. Wouldn't it, Georgia demanded, cut the ground out from under her if her own father were seen as opposition, wouldn't it make her seem less serious and more a child?

I thought Daddy's position a reasonable one. If the story were going to be told, it should *all* be told. Not everyone in town, not everyone in the same family, was obliged to feel identically about *anything,* and his point of view was just as valid and just as likely to interest people as Georgia's. After all, he reminded her, without fascists like himself, where would Georgia have found a battle worthy of her? This last, naturally, was accompanied by his familiar twisted, downturned smile.

One thing the members of the press did which no one in Owanka had thought to do was poll the citizenry. And the results of these daily tabulations kept Georgia's spirits high. According to what reporters called their "best information," the populace was almost evenly divided on the book. They noted the way in which churches had voted, and civic groups, but also wondered aloud about how people would behave once inside the voting booths, covered by blue bunting, hid-

den from the world, alone with their consciences. In
Georgia's mind the certainty grew that in those tiny,
enclosed spaces, almost like church confessionals, people would mark their ballots on the side of freedom.
There was simply no other choice.

Robin bussed down from Iowa City on Sunday evening in order to help Georgia mount her last big push,
to march in the parade, and to vote first thing on Tuesday morning before bussing back.

Mother had given Georgia one day off from school,
period. If she chose Monday, then she had to go back
on Tuesday, election day. Which made a certain amount
of sense because by then, what more could she do?

What Georgia accomplished on Monday was amazing. She was out of the house at dawn, meeting down
at the bank with Mr. Arrand and Laura McCandless,
planning the route of the parade which would move
from the high school into town, almost two and a half
miles' walk. They organized the evening's speakers,
arranging who was to follow whom on the podium,
worrying over delivery of loudspeaker equipment from
Iowa City, working on hand-painted banners and signs
for their followers, appointing marshals, filling balloons of red, white, and blue.

At five o'clock, an hour before the march was scheduled to begin, Georgia burst back into the house to
change into warmer clothes and to collect her speech,
on which she had been working off and on for the past
weeks. She bounded down the stairs from our room into
the living room, where Mother had set up a tray-table
for her. Father had come back from the store early and
was sitting in his easy chair there, drink in hand, as
Georgia dove into a plate of spaghetti.

"Is there time for you to give us a preview?" he asked
as Georgia stuffed herself in record time.

She shook her head and swallowed hugely. "You'll just have to come to the rally," she said without one trace of a grin.

"I plan to," Father said.

Georgia nodded curtly, all business.

"Georgia," Father started to say, "I want you to know that no matter what happens, you have my entire—"

"I don't want to hear it," Georgia said angrily, standing up and wiping her mouth with a paper napkin. "I don't want to hear one smarmy word! How my own father can see things this way I'll never know! But I don't want to know now. I give up! If what Ava wrote in *The Hawk* didn't make you change your mind, if Miss McCandless' being fired didn't do it, if Mr. Bracken's car being blown to bits didn't, then it's clear as can be that nothing can reach you! So just don't try condescending to me now!"

She grabbed her coat which was festooned with buttons and campaign badges and ran out of the room without looking back. That was probably a good thing, because I'm not certain that even Father's fabled even temper would have held under that barrage.

There was silence for a moment in the living room, and then we heard a shriek from Georgia outside.

We rushed to the front door and Father pulled it open. At the curbside, at the end of the walk, was Rick's car, battered and worn-looking and muddy, its front door open, Georgia's legs just disappearing into the front seat.

Father smiled and closed the door slowly, waving them off. He started back toward the living room, putting an arm over my shoulders. "You know, Ava, what Georgia said just now was pretty accurate. The piece you wrote for your newspaper almost did make me change my mind. I don't know if I told you how much I admired it."

"You didn't," I said quietly.

"Well, I did and I was very, very proud of you when I read it," he said.

"So was I," Mother echoed, standing in the hallway near the front closet, putting on her scarf and gloves and overcoat.

Since our house was halfway between downtown and school, we hadn't far to walk. Or to return, if we tired and wanted to, an option that appealed to me since the weather had grown cold and windy and snow flurries were forecast for the area. Jonny chose to stay at home, saying simply, "I'll probably see you all on T.V. later."

As we neared the athletic field behind Owanka High, we could hear the murmurs of the crowd, a steady hum that rose and fell and rose again. But I'd no idea how big the crowd would be until we rounded a corner of the building and looked down past the bleachers. There must have been a thousand people there! Old people, middle-aged, young kids, parents, teens in gangs. Mr. Arrand and Georgia and Miss McCandless milled among the throng, distributing buttons and streamers and balloons and banners, encouraging their troops, smiling and laughing and giving thumbs-up signs in the gathering darkness. All of a sudden, a whistle was blown and obediently people became silent and maneuvered into position.

The march began, flashlights and burning torches held in the air, banners blowing in the breeze, campaign badges and buttons reflecting the firelight. There was an atmosphere of expectation and the thrill of being surrounded by so many people who believed and cared as we did, and whenever a television cameraman's lights played over the marchers, shouts rose and arms waved in the air and people started chanting, "Freedom Is Reading Is Freedom, Freedom Is Reading Is Freedom!"

None of the three of us felt compelled to march in the front ranks. We walked arm in arm amid the mob, located about a third of the way back in the train. I squeezed my father's arm and teased him. "Spy, that's what you are! Benedict Arnold!"

He simply smiled. He knew what he would do when *he* got inside the blue velvet curtains the next morning. What did he care?

My mother, on the other side of him, was chanting along with the rest of Georgia's supporters, "Freedom Is Reading Is Freedom Is Reading," and so on, her voice reaching an easy sing-along within perhaps five hundred yards of the school. She looked very beautiful to me, her face flushed, her eyes bright, and I thought I saw in her what my father must have seen twenty years earlier.

We had gone about a mile when Robin appeared from behind us where, one assumed, he was hurrying along the laggards in the crush. He smiled and waved and touched my shoulder as he passed, scurrying to catch up to Georgia and Mr. Arrand in front. We still had seen nothing more of Rick.

We were perhaps a half mile from the town square when we saw the opposition, much of it silent, lining the roadway. As we passed, many of them nodded silently at friends or family members. But there was no other greeting. I thought I caught a glimpse of Darryl von Vrock's red hair at one curbside, and beside him, Sandra Balin. I smiled to myself. They deserved each other.

Then I noticed that a lot of these bystanders turned to follow our trail. I couldn't tell whether they did so out of curiosity or a desire to intimidate. I noticed a few placards then, most having to do with abortion and Right to Life movements, and a few anti-ERA posters above a half-dozen heads.

Our gang rounded a corner and found itself in the center of the square, being drawn magnetically to the steps of City Hall, its white columns lit by floodlights as well as the smaller, more precise lights of television cameramen. A stage had been erected there on the steps and it was lined with red, white, and blue bunting and balloons. Microphones stood ready and switched on and when Donald Arrand mounted the few steps to stand before us and raised his hands over his head, the roar that erupted from the crowd in the square rang out to be amplified by them, and then to ring back in our ears from the loudspeakers strategically placed around the approach to City Hall.

The chanting of "Freedom Is Reading Is Freedom" continued for a minute or so more. I looked around the square and saw we were surrounded by hundreds of other people clearly not in sympathy with our cause. Then Rick materialized and put his arms around me. I looked up at him. His eyes were alight, and he was certainly not feeling any antagonism toward Georgia's squadrons.

"I thought you agreed with Father," I said into his ear.

He looked at me with wide eyes. "How'd you know?"

I grinned. "What does it matter? The point is, you're on the other side. What are you doing here?"

"I came to vote," Rick said. "Georgia doesn't have to know how I feel. Besides, I'm really impressed with all this. Maybe she'll win and then she won't care."

"And then what?" I half-shouted up at him. "Are you going back?" He seemed puzzled. "Or are you waiting till the end of the semester?" I added.

"You belong in the C.I.A." Rick laughed.

"Well?" I nudged him.

But he wouldn't be nudged. "I'm still thinking," he

said over the noise of the crowd. "And you're not helping me."

Mr. Arrand was warming up the crowd, and we both tuned in to listen. "Now, I know," he was saying, "that people have tried to confuse the issue here. Have tried to make those of us who favor the freedom of children to read into Godless, pro-abortion wastrels of the public purse. But we stand here tonight simply to show them, and anyone else who may be watching, what freedom really means. It includes the right of assembly!" There was a solid wall of applause erected here. "It includes the right of choice, whether that choice be religious or political or personal!" More applause. "It affirms the professionalism of our teachers and leaders of our young who want only to be allowed to do the best possible job under what are frequently the least advantageous of circumstances!" Still more applause.

Even Father applauded politely, clapping his gloved hands a few times and nodding as though he had been in agreement all along. I looked at him quickly and punched his elbow. He leaned toward my ear. "He's right, after all. Freedom does include those things."

I nodded at his explanation. *God, this is what's called being secure,* I thought.

Georgia assumed Mr. Arrand's place at the microphone and modestly stood waiting for the crowd to quiet. She did nothing but stand absolutely still, a nice smile on her face, waiting. When we had all ceased talking among ourselves and waving flags, she took one more step toward the microphone. With her arms still at her sides, and without gestures, she spoke into the bulb of the microphone clearly. Her voice sounded very, very young, but also idealistic, determined, jubilant.

If you would," she began, "you might repeat after

me a sort of pledge I believe all supporters of FIRIF can support." She paused.

Her voice grew stronger. "I am an American," she began. "An American is free to choose..." She waited, and after a hesitant start the crowd collectively agreed to follow her direction. It was amazing.

"...where he lives," Georgia said. The crowd echoed her.

"...with whom he lives."

"With whom he lives."

"...at what he works and where."

"At what he works and where."

"...to worship in his own church."

"To worship in his own church."

"...his own friends and neighbors."

"His own friends and neighbors."

"...to speak the ideas of his mind, and the longings of his heart."

"To speak the ideas of his mind, and the longings of his heart."

"...to profit by the lessons of others."

"To profit by the lessons of others."

"...and to learn to live, to love, to be an American from any source he can."

"And to learn to live, to love, to be an American from any source he can."

"Thank you very much," said Georgia then, backing away from the microphone and sitting down.

There was a second's silence and then a thunderous cry erupted from us all. I cheered and stamped and clapped, and all the time kept saying to myself, *Brady hasn't got a chance, Brady hasn't got a prayer!*

Louise Nichols took the microphone next. "I won't take much of your time," she said. "It's too chilly."

Applause and "Right ons!"

"Before we introduce the candidates for City Council

we support, and who support FIRIF, I want to tell you this country got where it is by keeping its eye on the ball. And that's what we're doing here tonight. We don't want to argue with our friends about economics or national prestige. All we want is the right of our children to learn about the world."

Agreeable nods and applause from the crowd.

Mrs. Nichols smiled out and nodded. "What we want is clean, moral, and honest. It's called Freedom!"

More applause, though by that time I began to think I couldn't take much more emotion in any form.

Mrs. Nichols then introduced the eight candidates from the slate of twenty FIRIF endorsed. As the last candidate (Amos Allen) resumed his seat, Laura McCandless stepped to the microphone. There was a rush of whispering and then applause which started slowly and built. Had we all been seated, we probably would have risen to our feet just then. She waited patiently, smiling, looking astonishingly pretty—do public meetings make all women blossom?—and competent and cool. After a moment she raised her hands just a little to ask that the applause stop, and it did.

"My name," she said clearly, "is Laura McCandless. I was librarian at Owanka High."

She couldn't have stopped the crowd had she wanted; another round of fervent applause broke out.

"I stayed on here in Owanka to vote tomorrow," she said finally.

*More* applause.

"I am not a martyr. None of us here is. All I am is a citizen of this country who expects that the guarantees in our Constitution reach out to include herself. As they do you...and your children."

Applause.

"We at Owanka High take, or took, our responsibil-

ities seriously. We examined and read every book we
recommended or approved or bought. We brought the
best and clearest sets of standards we could to these
decisions, teachers and librarians alike. As professionals, we want to do our job well, we want to help initiate
children into a meaningful and worthwhile adulthood."

She smiled then and I was relieved. Suddenly things
had turned too heavy.

"The freedom to read is a precious one," she said
after a moment. Her voice began to quaver. "Don't let
angry, ambitious, ignorant people take it away from
you *or* your children!"

One or two people started to clap, but Miss Mc-
Candless was not finished. She was shaking now, and
tears were beginning to fall from her eyes.

"No matter how hard we try," she said, almost shouting now, "in the face of prejudice and racism and in-
tolerance, we cannot fight alone!" Her shoulders were
heaving now. I held my breath. "Don't let this country
down! Don't give in to hate-mongers! Don't give in to
ambitious, unprincipled demagogues who try to make
you afraid and ashamed to exercise your rights as
Americans!"

There was total silence as Miss McCandless slumped
back into the shadows and stood before her chair, sob-
bing uncontrollably.

I'm not willing to swear that *my* next few seconds
were unique, but this is what they contained: *No wonder she's a wreck. She's lost her job, been threatened
and bullied. Stood up to it all. She had to crack sometime. There* is *a difference between the abstract and the
personal. She's been mutilated by all this. Here is
Owanka's first walking wounded. The poor woman.*

I tore off my gloves as quickly as I could and started
to clap. Not to cheer on what Miss McCandless had said
but to send her a message that someone in the crowd

understood her pain and was sympathetic. Other people apparently had reached the same state as I because my hands were not the only ones so occupied. It took a while to start but we few generated support and respect and happily, before too long, the air was full of the sound of hands applauding. There were no cheers, no shouts. This reaction was more dignified, more aware, more purposeful than your usual hoopla. The ovation continued. Mr. Arrand stepped toward the microphone and then abruptly turned back away from it again, motioning for Miss McCandless to come forward. She did, but reluctantly, standing at his side, his arm about her waist drawing her in, unable to look directly out at us all. There were still tears streaming down her cheeks.

Our hands would not be stopped. Finally, after what seemed a very long and emotional time, Miss McCandless was allowed to turn away from Mr. Arrand and to disappear once more into the shadows at the back of the stage. Then Georgia and Mrs. Nichols joined Mr. Arrand at the microphone. They seemed to be speaking in unison, and we could not at first hear their words, which were, "My country, 'tis of thee, Sweet land of liberty." But by the time they had reached "Of thee I sing," we were with them. The anthem rose through the night air and seemed weighted with what perhaps was the first realization of the crowd collected there that we were, indeed, in a battle for part of our freedom. The singing was solemn, not elated, and when, at the end of the song, Mr. Arrand stepped forward and leaned down into the microphone to say, "Thank you all for coming," we knew how terrible war could be.

# 24.

"I am going into the kitchen," Father announced, "and make as much popcorn as the biggest pan will hold. I am going to melt a pound of butter. And I'm going to come back in here and offer it to you. You had better be smiling."

"Fat chance," said Mother under her breath. Then she smiled. "I'll do it, Fred," she said, standing up from the couch. "You stay and watch the returns."

"Ohhhh, Alva," said Father.

"Don't you ohhh, Alva me," Mother replied quickly. She and Daddy exchanged looks and then both laughed. Mother left and we heard her rummaging around the kitchen for the big pot we keep for boiling vegetables in, which also doubles as our popcorn maker whenever Daddy gets hit by one of his insatiable seizures.

He and I sat then, switching between a local (sort of) station for state and city returns, and John Chancellor. Rick and Robin had both returned to their schools. They had voted as soon as the polls were open, come home for breakfast, and then taken off. Georgia was God knows where, although we all knew where she really *was:* Mr. Arrand's house, anticipating victory.

I had been late for supper, going with Martin at five

to pick up his belongings at the Ellis house. It seemed all of Owanka had voted early, and there were projections of the outcome on the car's radio already. While the real issue over *The Grapes of Wrath* was still in doubt, the races for the Council seemed to have been decided quickly. Martin's father was out.

Martin didn't seem terribly upset about his father's loss, but he did feel that no matter which side won, when someone in a family was down, you rallied round. I agreed.

"You were in a bit of a pickle there for a while, too, you know," Martin said to me.

"What do you mean?"

He grinned. "Letting yourself be hounded by von Vrock."

Naturally, having felt guilty about this before, I overreacted. "Well, *you* certainly didn't give any indication you cared very much about it."

"What did you want me to do?" Martin asked. "Break his legs? Cut a cable on his car?"

"I don't know," I said weakly. "It just seems to me that if you cared the way you say, you would have... rescued me."

Martin laughed. "You didn't want that," he said. "You wanted to toy and tease and see what the new boy had to offer. Come on, Ave, admit it. You may not have been serious about him, but you were curious."

I blushed.

"So," Martin urged, taking one of my hands, "what did you find out?"

I shrugged. This was not my most articulate hour.

He folded me into his arms, where, I admit, I was glad to be. "Never mind," he whispered in my ear. "I admit I was a little nervous, a little worried. And if I'd thought there was any danger of losing you to that

creep, I *would* have rescued you. I would have had to,
for both of us."

We kissed. I was glad of that, too.

By the time I got home, the television set was on in
the living room and more national projections were in
the air. We flipped from network to local stations, and
I admit it's rather exciting hearing the returns from
your very own town on statewide channels. My father
was in charge of the controls, and he dialed around to
see Walter Cronkite. "I'll miss him when he's gone,"
he said. "This is his last election."

"Daddy, he's not dying, you know."

"Still," he said, "I feel as though he's been with me
all my adult life. As a matter of fact, he has."

I smiled and sat without moving, listening to the
returns. The volume was set loud enough so Mother in
the kitchen could hear, and every so often, when a
liberal senator had been declared the loser to a new
conservative candidate, she groaned loudly. We switched
to ABC, to Frank Reynolds and Barbara Walters.

"Can I come down?" Jonny yelled.

"No," replied Father firmly. "Tomorrow's a school
day, and you already know who's going to be President."

"I can smell popcorn!" Jonny shouted.

"It's bad for your digestion!" Father yelled back. "Go
back to bed. I'll bring you some when it's ready."

Jonny's feet padded over our heads.

"You know," I said tentatively, "I begin to think
maybe I'm ready for the world out there."

"Whoever doubted it?" asked Father kindly.

I shrugged. "Me, I guess. It's funny. Rick goes off
with all flags flying and finds out he doesn't like it, or
at least that he's not ready to face it yet. I think I am."

Father, who had finally been brought into Rick's
confused confidences after the rally, had surprised him

and me and all of us by being positively philosophic about the whole thing. He did not change now. "There are right times and wrong ones. I respect Rick for recognizing the difference. Also, I admit, but only to you, Ava, that I hope he'll change his mind. Not for me, *honestly*. But for himself. I can't help thinking that college *does* make a difference, now and in the future."

"Well," I said, not really knowing what was going to come out of my mouth, "I think I'm ready to be tested. Ready to have to make choices, to learn to pick and choose."

"I'm sure you will be, sweetheart," Father said.

"Will be what?" asked Mother, bringing in the popcorn pot and placing it on the coffee table in front of us.

"Tested," Daddy said, reaching out for a handful of popcorn. "We were talking about Rick's situation at school."

"Oh," said Mother, her brows crinkling unhappily. "I just wish he'd change his mind."

"I can still smell it!" Jonny shouted from his bed.

"I'm coming, I'm coming!" Father called back. "Keep your shirt on!" He stood up and went to the kitchen quickly, returning with a cereal bowl he scooped into the pot, and then left to take it up to Jonny.

Mother watched the screen a moment. "You know, I am absolutely baffled at some of the people who seem to have gotten onto the Council."

"You are?"

She nodded, switching channels again to a Davenport station. "I can understand returning Irene Clarke. And I'm pleased Louise Nichols scraped by. And even Stanley Sopwith, bless his soul. *And* I mean that!" Mother laughed. "The poor man, taken over by the rabid right. He won't be able to move without finding a sword in his ribs."

"It's not as though he doesn't deserve it," I said. "You know, there isn't any sex between animals and human beings in that book."

"I know that."

"I wonder why no one ever called him on it."

"How many people would go to the trouble of reading the book?" Mother asked in return.

"Any sympathy for Mr. Brady?" I asked slyly.

My mother looked at me sideways. "Not a whit!" she said then, but after a second she laughed. "Fairchild doesn't need to be on the Council anyway. He's got more than enough influence in this town."

"Still, I wonder why he lost."

"The same reason, partly, that Amos Allen lost. People like change," Mother said. "Also, in Fairchild's case, I think he made a mistake trying to stay above the battle. I mean, after all, *he* started it. You can't do something like that and then pretend that to be involved is somehow lower-class."

"I think pushing Miss McCandless hurt him, too," I suggested as Mother got up to switch channels to one from Iowa City.

We watched in silence. The reporters talked about the early presidential decision, about our governor's being re-elected, and then about state and local issues. Suddenly, on the screen, we saw the Owanka proposition illustrated. The station must have had a direct line into City Hall, because as each ballot was tallied, it appeared on the screen. In a word, we were losing. The vote, at that time, was something like 650 for the proposition, and 610 against it. Mother and I looked at each other but said nothing. There didn't seem to be anything we *could* say. We were probably both thinking about Georgia.

We watched a while more, munching occasionally on the popcorn. Then, without warning, the front door

slammed, startling us both. We turned around quickly
and saw Georgia on the threshold. Her face was tear-
streaked and terribly pale, and she was trembling.

"Darling!" Mother said, standing up quickly and
starting toward her.

"Where's Father?" Georgia demanded.

"On my way down," he said, coming down the stair-
case.

Georgia shrugged off her parka and threw it on the
floor, taking a few steps into the living room.

"Well?" she shouted. "Are you happy?"

Father came into the room and stood a moment, looking solemnly at her. "Not to see you this way, sweetheart."

"Well, you made me this way!" Georgia cried out,
gesturing at herself.

Father made an attempt to go to her and embrace
her but she sidestepped him.

He stopped. "I certainly had a hand in making you,"
Father admitted, "but at a certain point, one should be
old enough to accept responsibility for what one is."

"Oh, smooth!" Georgia declared. "That's the whole
trouble, all the way through this thing; you've been so
laid back, so cool. You're exactly like the others."

Father smiled. "No better, no worse," he decided.
"You know, you haven't lost by a landslide, darling.
It's very close. You did a spectacular job."

"But don't you realize what you've done?" Georgia
asked. "You voted against democracy!"

Father crossed the living room and sat down in front
of the popcorn bowl. Reaching into it, he said, "Listen
to yourself, please, Miss Van Buren. I voted—*in* a democracy. Pure and simple. I did my civic duty, gladly,
proudly. Other people voted as I did, and some differently. But what you're so steamed up about is that

democracy has just shown you it can contain ideas *you* don't approve of."

"Georgia," Mother said sweetly, "just stop a minute and think what you've done. Think what you were able to accomplish. There ought to be some pleasure in that."

Georgia spun. "Well, there isn't!" she announced.

Mother shook her head. "I'm sorry about that, then, sweetheart. Really. You have won the respect of *so* many people."

Georgia dismissed that quickly. "I don't think I can live in a house where people don't believe in freedom."

Father smiled.

"Stop that!" Georgia shouted. "Just stop! It's not funny!"

"Yes, it is," Father told her. "After all, your mother voted as you wanted."

"Of course she did!" Georgia said. "She at least has brains and a sense of history."

"And I don't," Father asked without adding a question mark.

"How can you?" Georgia demanded. "Anyone could see that what was at stake here was continuing what America is based on. I mean, you're so all-fired hot to return to the good old days, you forgot what the good old days were."

"I'm not sure that's true," said Father. "And you are perilously close, Georgia, to being offensive."

Georgia lowered her voice, a little. "*I'*m sure," she said, stomping then across the room to gather a handful of popcorn. "How, just how, and why, do you think the Van Burens ever came over here anyway?"

Father shrugged. "I imagine some of their friends talked them into it."

"Well, I certainly hope not!" Georgia snorted. "I hope at least someone in this family understood what was going on."

"Do I understand, dear," Mother asked, "that you attribute the acceptance of Mr. Brady's proposal directly to your father?"

"I most certainly do!" Georgia said firmly. "After all, everything he's ever told us, taught us should have shown him what mattered. He could have helped us instead of standing silently by, like some gigantic statue too smug and smart for its own britches. He could have joined us, talked to his friends, talked to people who came into the store!"

"People come in to buy things, Georgia," said Father. "Not for advice."

"Besides," I put in, "no matter how upset you are, the vote isn't lopsided. A lot of people did agree with you."

"I can't be bothered with your numbers game!" Georgia declared.

"It's very difficult to discuss this with you, then, dear," Mother judged, "when no matter what we say, or how much sense it makes, you always have an answer."

"Well, what do you expect?" Georgia demanded. "I've just spent almost three months of my life, my whole *youth*, fighting for what I believe in!"

"It was a good fight," Father said kindly. "You've nothing to be ashamed of. You nearly won."

"I am *not* ashamed!" Georgia announced. "Far from it. I'm going to fight for the rest of my life."

"For what?" I asked. "For this, a *book?*"

Georgia shook her head. "No, I'm going to fight every time I see people being forced against a wall, being mistreated, being bullied by power and influence and money."

"Darling, other people know how to fight those same things," Father put in. "You don't have to do it all alone."

"I know that!" Georgia snapped. "If nothing else, all this has shown me I'm *not* alone, even though my very own family wouldn't support me."

"I did," I said. "Mother did, Robin did."

"That's not what I mean," Georgia returned. "Anyone who grew up in America, who ever learned about life and liberty and the pursuit of happiness should have backed me."

"That depends on one's pursuit," Father judged. "Some of us go at things a little less fervently than you."

Georgia ignored him. "I will *not* let someone else plan my life, make decisions for me."

"I don't believe we've ever tried to do that, dear," Mother said.

"Maybe not on purpose," Georgia relented, "but you sure have. I mean, what's the point of having children if it isn't to duplicate yourselves, duplicate the way you see things and feel and behave?"

Father smiled as he reached back into the popcorn bowl. "Oddly enough, there's supposed to be an element of pleasure in having children, too."

"Pleasure!" shrieked Georgia. "Pleasure? When you publicly humiliate and belittle them?"

"Georgia," Father said severely, "we haven't done that. We've never done that."

"That's what *you* say!" It was true, what Mother had said—this was a no-win argument. "And you may as well know right now that this battle isn't over, not by a long shot! Mr. Arrand says we can take this to court, we can appeal, find it unconstitutional. And that's exactly what we're going to do! Other people have. Other towns have. So," Georgia said, scooping up her parka and getting ready to leave the room, turning to make her curtain speech, "from now on I'm on my own! You can advise and talk and worry, but I'm no longer a child! And you'd better realize that!"

Mother looked at Daddy as Georgia ran upstairs. "Has there been much doubt of that lately?" she asked him.

"Well," I said, sinking down onto the couch and rustling popcorn from under Daddy's nose, "Georgia sure doesn't plan a sneak attack."

My father smiled his curious smile. "Of course, Alva, *we* have not yet begun to fight."

"God, Fred, if you tell Georgia that, she'll murder you in your sleep!"

Father laughed. "It wouldn't be much fun for her if she didn't have opposition."

"Oh Lord," my mother sighed. "I thought I knew my family!"

"I'm teasing, honey," Father said then.

"Thank God for that!" Mother said happily, but with just a trace of worry still in her voice.

"Well, she's all yours," I announced, standing up. I don't know why I felt compelled to stand. I just did. "I'm going out in the world to see what other battles are being fought."

Mother smiled. Then she laughed softly. "From what we've just heard, darling, you can explore and you can chart new territories. But if I know Georgia—and I admit I may not, after all this—if you ever run into another war, don't be too surprised to find her in the front lines."

I nodded and smiled a little. "Somewhere behind me."